Collection

Book 1

OLIVIA BENNETT
ILLUSTRATED BY GEORGIA RUCKER

Created by Biscotti Books
Illustrated by Georgia Rucker

Published by Sourcebooks Jabberwocky, an imprint of Sourcebooks, Inc.
P.O. Box 4410, Naperville, Illinois 60567-4410
(630) 961-3900
Fax: (630) 961-2168
www.jabberwockykids.com

Library of Congress Cataloging-in-Publication data is on file with the publisher.

Source of Production: Versa Press, East Peoria, Illinois, USA
Date of Production: October 2010
Run Number: 13609

Printed and bound in the United States of America.
VP 10 9 8 7 6 5 4 3 2 1

With special thanks
to Sherri Rifkin

"Fashion is not something that exists in dresses only. Fashion is in the sky, in the street; fashion has to do with ideas, the way we live, what is happening."

—*Coco Chanel*

THE GAME

Definitely the faux-fur scarf. But not in teal…maybe an eggplant with silver flecks would work.

She quickly sketched the scarf onto the heavy white paper. As her pencil danced across the page, the whole world faded away. At least for a minute or two.

She glanced up, scanning the breathing-room-only subway car. Person to person, outfit to outfit, her eyes jumped around like a robotic scanning device in a science-fiction movie. Colors, patterns, fabrics, textures, and shapes leaped out at her. Turquoise set against a rich chocolate brown. A collar the same acid-green color and gnarly texture of Oscar the Grouch. A perfectly cut A-line skirt that hit just the right place, where the thigh curves in slightly. Black over hot-pink tights. She never stopped at the faces. It wasn't about the faces. It was all about the clothes.

Always had been.

She couldn't always remember people's names, but she could describe the outfit they were wearing when she met them—down to the shape of the buttons—without having to think for a single second. Her mother loved to tell about the time when she was three or four and said, "I want the baby-sitter with the violet halter top, the skirt that looks like it was made out of jeans, and the triangle heels on her shoes." She loved wedges even before she knew what they were.

The sound of the doors snapping shut shook her from her daydreams. She only had two more stops to finish the Game. People jostled into the packed car, causing a man in a stained tan overcoat to roll his eyes with annoyance as he grasped the pole. She actually liked it when the subway car was crowded. The more people, the more outfits she could choose from for the Game.

The object of the Game was deceptively simple: Choose separate items of clothing from different people on the subway to create a fashion "wow." Colors could be changed, and silhouettes altered a bit. The resulting outfit had to be one that she would wear—well, that is if she were going someplace more fabulous than middle school.

It was a game of skill *and* speed: She had to complete the challenge before the subway reached her stop. And at this time of the morning, the city's resident fashionistas hadn't even sipped their first lattes, much less stepped a stiletto onto the subway, which made scoring points that much harder.

A burst of laughter drew her attention down the aisle. Three college-aged girls circled closely around the same silver pole, chatting loudly to one another as if they were at a party. The tallest of the three wore a military-like flack jacket.

Perfect! If she changed the drab green to a sleeker steel blue, it would totally work. Her pencil flew into overdrive. As she sketched, she slimmed the cut to create a more feminine, less bulky shape. All she needed now was a bottom of some kind to add to her half-dressed female figure.

The subway stopped, and the doors opened. People pushed out and more piled in, revealing a fresh batch of new fashion candidates. Suddenly, a college girl with a side ponytail leaped through the closing doors, just making it before they caught her in their unforgiving death grip. She wore the most fabulous pair of cherry-red patent leather boots.

OMG
shiny
patent
leather

They must be vintage, Emma thought. She could tell by their shape—low, boxy heels and squared-off toes—and their quality. The patent leather looked real, not fake and plasticky. True, they weren't pants, but she could still make the boots work.

With seconds to spare, she added them to her sketch and then linked the jacket to the awesome boots with simple bold lines to stand in for basic black leggings.

Finished!

She gazed at her newest creation. The outfit's bold charcoal lines contrasted with the stark white of the paper. Later, she'd pull out her colored pencils and Pantone markers to fill in the lines according to the color notes she'd made in the margins. She'd fiddle a little more to make the outfit even better. Maybe make the scarf longer or the jacket skinnier or even stretch it out into a short dress.

The train jerked to a halt. Closing her sketchbook, this one bound in amethyst Chinese brocade, she tucked it safely into her bag.

The Game was over.

Time for school.

THE POWER OF CLOTHES

Emma Rose pushed open the school's heavy red door in a fashion-induced haze, mentally creating, designing, and storing scraps of ideas the way she imagined mathematicians juggled numbers or chefs mixed ingredients. The Downtown Day School halls were in their usual state of pre-homeroom pandemonium.

Following the tide of self-confident eighth graders and somehow still-clueless sixth graders, she quickly inventoried the outfits of the day. Baggy sweatshirts. Colorful tanks under hoodies. Jeans. More jeans. Even more jeans. The halls of Downtown Day would never be confused with the catwalks of a couture show. That was for sure.

Emma turned the corner, and a whiff of watermelon suddenly hit her. She smiled. Holly was waiting by their lockers. The fruity gum scent was a dead giveaway.

"Cool sweater," Holly Richardson said, after popping an almost-fluorescent pink bubble.

"Thanks." Emma wore a black cotton cardigan, on which

she had replaced the plain plastic buttons with shiny brass marching-band uniform buttons. She liked to have fun with fashion—to create mash-ups of vintage and thrift-store finds.

She mixed in the occasional trendier bargain—but always gave those items her personal touch. When she went for a pair of ballet flats, she opted for Kelly green and clipped a pair of sparkly rhinestone earrings onto the toe to make them different. She even replaced the drawstring in her charcoal velour sweatpants with a shimmery chartreuse ribbon.

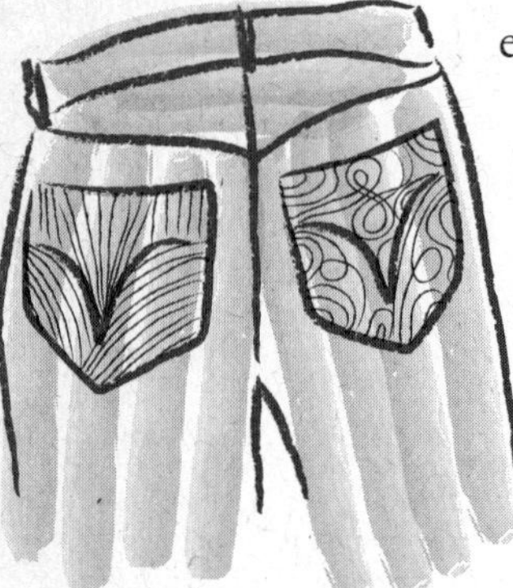

Although she did it quietly, and often quite subtly, Emma wore something every day that hinted at her unique personal sense of style. She might twist colorful silk scarves into a belt or drape them around her neck in a heap. Or she might wear a boyish flannel shirt with the cuffs turned up to show off a purple satin lining she'd sewn in. Her worn-out boys' Levi's were a wardrobe staple—she

loved the design she'd embroidered onto the back pockets with metallic thread. It made her happy when Holly noticed her little fashion statements.

"But what's with the ponytail?" Holly sized up Emma's shoulder-length dark-brown hair in the way only a best friend would.

Emma self-consciously tucked a strand back into her messy ponytail. "What do you mean?"

Holly shrugged. "Nothing. It's just that you wear it like that *every* day."

"So?" Emma was much more interested in figuring out what she was going to wear than wrestling with a blow dryer and humongous brush like Holly had suddenly started doing every morning.

Holly popped another bubble. "All I'm saying is that it could probably look a lot cuter if you styled it out or something. I mean, with the awesome outfits you're always putting together, it just doesn't seem to go. That's all."

Emma bit her lip. She knew Holly was trying to help, but these days beauty advice was hard to hear from her. Every time Emma saw Holly, she was surprised by her friend's transformation. When the two girls first met—back in Miss Judy's preschool—they had been exactly the same height, and they were line buddies for years because of that.

But then last year Holly had shot up five inches without gaining an ounce, it seemed. Now, with her long, thick, honey-brown wavy hair, blue eyes, clear skin, and pretty smile, she looked like the kind of girl who would be spotted on the street by an agent and become a supermodel overnight. If they hadn't been best friends since the days of finger painting and macaroni necklaces, Emma would've probably been too intimidated to talk to Holly now.

Compared with Holly, Emma thought that she was boring-looking. Not gorgeous, not ugly, just in between. She did have bright green eyes, which she got from her dad, and what her grandmother called her "sweet smile," but what set Emma apart were clothes. She understood their power. How they could transform a person. Even her. It didn't matter how messy your ponytail looked, if you sported a flirty minidress or high suede boots.

By contrast, Holly's look was cool and classic. Holly's mom was one of those people who believed in buying very, very good things that would last a very, very long time. Holly's outfit was typical Holly: dark jeans, soft chocolate-brown flats, a thin lemon-colored sweater, and a stretchy wrap T-shirt underneath. As always, she looked as if she had stepped out of the pages of a preppy catalog. As much as Emma begged her, Holly never took fashion risks.

"A bunch of us are going to hang out in the park after school." Holly unwrapped a second piece of gum and popped it in her mouth. "Can you come with?"

Emma could guess exactly who "a bunch of us" were. Ivana Abbott and the "Ivana-Bees"—as in "I Wanna Be Ivana"—Lexie Blackburn, Kayla Levine, and Shannon O'Malley.

"Will Number One, Number Two, and Number Three be there, too?" she asked, hoping for a giggle from Holly. Until recently, she and Holly had referred to the Ivana-Bees by number because, even though they looked different, they acted exactly the same, laughing at everything Ivana said and doing whatever she wanted whenever she wanted.

Instead, Holly looked slightly offended. "Come on, Em. Don't pretend you don't know their names. They're really nice, you know. Just give them a chance."

"I still don't know how you can be friends with Ivana," Emma said. "She actually created a *fan* page for herself on Facebook, like she's famous or something. I mean, give me a break."

Holly laughed. "Oh, come on. It's kind of cool. Like those reviews she does of movies and CDs and all those amazing restaurants she goes to with her parents? They're hilarious!"

Emma used all her self-control to not roll her eyes. She couldn't wait for the day when Ivana would become bored with Holly and move on—or even better, the other way around—so that it would be just Emma and Holly again. But that hadn't happened yet. In fact, it looked like Holly was currently applying for the position of Number Four.

"Just come with us. What's the big deal?" Holly persisted.

"I'm not sure if I can today," Emma said as she opened her locker. Her tiny metal sanctuary. She had lined the inside of the door with a swatch of 1970s Marimekko fabric in a great green-and-white graphic print. Large square magnets covered in random fabric swatches held clippings from various fashion magazines. The framed picture of her style hero, the one and only Coco Chanel, hung in the center of her rotating fashion collage.

Seeing Coco's face every day reminded Emma that there was a whole world outside these walls, a world filled with stunningly beautiful dresses made of luxurious fabrics, intricately detailed jackets, expertly tailored pants and skirts, and, of course, killer shoes and bags.

"Some guys are coming, including Jackson Creedon,"

Holly singsonged, knowing that she had just majorly sweetened the deal.

Emma was no math genius, but even she could calculate that Jackson being there added much more to the equation than Ivana took away. Emma turned to face her friend. "Are you serious?"

"Would I lie about that? *Hello!* Have you met me?"

Emma had been crushing on Jackson Creedon ever since he had stepped foot into school three weeks earlier. Maybe it was his intense blue eyes or the way his brown wavy hair, which was on the long side, kept flopping into his face or the fact that he was taller than the other boys and lean—strong but not all thick-necked and muscle-y.

At the end of the first week, Holly had declared Emma officially infatuated. Emma could hardly deny it, even though she and Jackson had never exchanged a single word. Yet. But going to the park could change all that…maybe he would actually notice her.

Emma groaned. "Sorry, Holls, but I really can't go. I just remembered that I promised my dad I'd work for him after school."

Underneath her fringy bangs, Holly's eyes narrowed, the way they always did when she was preparing to get her way. "You're picking *lace* over Jackson Creedon? Can't you just do it tomorrow?"

"I wish." Emma sighed. "But it has to be today because they're getting in a big shipment that needs to be unpacked, and there aren't enough people to help out."

Emma had started working for Noah—as Emma called her dad at Laceland, his wholesale lace business—during the summer. When school started, she had agreed to work in the afternoons to earn extra money for design materials without having to be stuck home baby-sitting her ten-year-old brother, William. But today, when her best friend and the hot new guy were hanging in the park, having an after-school job was a bummer.

"Plus," Emma added, "I kind of need the money."

"For what?" Holly demanded, gum snapping and cracking.

"I'm working on the most amazing dress. The fabric cost a lot."

Holly nodded slowly, clearly unhappy that Emma was not going to the park.

"Besides," Emma said, "doesn't Lexie have a thing for Jackson? Even if I could go, she'd never let me get anywhere near him."

Holly waved her hand. "Just because Lexie likes Jackson doesn't mean he likes her back. He's new to school. I bet if he got to know you, he'd like you much more than Lexie."

Emma allowed a small smile. She appreciated Holly's pep talk, but they both knew that a guy would have to be blind not to be drawn to Lexie's exotic looks. Long dark-brown, perfectly smooth, straight hair; almond skin; dark-brown eyes with a perfect veil of mascara-enhanced lashes. It was a killer combination.

"Look, you'll never know whether or not he's going to like you unless you come." Holly closed her locker. "And I know how badly you want to know. So see you later, *right?*"

"Right," Emma found herself agreeing. Holly always had that effect on her.

"I mean, could there be a better excuse to skip work than getting to hang out with Jackson?" Holly smiled.

"Can't think of any," Emma said, as they made their way together upstairs toward first period. "Besides, how bad could it be to miss one measly afternoon at Laceland?"

Later that afternoon, as Emma stepped into the elevator of the century-old building that was home to Laceland, her mind was thirty blocks south in Washington Square Park. As the day wore on, she had realized that as much as she would trade a pair of Alexander McQueen shoes—that is, if she magically owned a pair—for the chance to hang out with Jackson, she couldn't break her promise to her dad. She was wired that way.

Now that she was here, it was blindingly obvious that she had made a crucial mistake. Jackson is probably talking to Lexie this very minute, Emma thought, a pit of regret growing in her stomach. Sometimes she wished there was a manual for all this boy stuff. Lexie and Ivana seemed to have it. For all she knew, they had written it themselves.

It was too late now.

The old elevator wobbled up past a handful of other textile importers, a zipper maker, an umbrella company, a hanger supplier, and a hosiery wholesaler, and then jerked to a stop on the eleventh floor. Emma walked down the windowless, dingy gray hallway and entered the reception area of Laceland.

The cavernous raw space with sixteen-foot ceilings had rows and rows of shelving, blocking out most of the light from the windows. Although the place was scrubbed once a week by a cleaning crew, a thin layer of dust blanketed Laceland from all the fabrics and trimmings that had passed through the warehouse over the past four decades, which was how long her dad's family had owned the business. Emma always stifled the urge to sneeze whenever she arrived.

"Honey! You're here. Hall-e-lujah!" Marjorie Kornbluth stood up from behind the Formica-covered reception desk, reaching for her purse.

"Excited to see me?" Emma teased.

"Am I *ever!* The phone hasn't stopped ringing all day," Marjorie complained in her scratchy, low rasp. "I need a real cup of coffee, not the black muck your father makes." She brushed past Emma in a cloud of eau de coffee and hair spray—her signature scent—and hurried into the waiting elevator, leaving Emma to take over her post.

"Have fun!" Emma called after her.

Even though that was usually the extent of their conversations, Emma adored Marjorie. She was a Laceland institution. She might actually have been working there longer than Emma's parents had been married. Marjorie was one of those ladies who seemed to be stuck in another era—when false eyelashes, sparkly shadow, and pink frosted lipstick were all the rage.

Every day, no matter what time of year, Marjorie wore only simple, black shift dresses. Her short bobbed hair was dyed platinum blond and had been that way forever. The only thing that had ever changed about her was the appearance of the tiniest lines on her pale, pale skin, increasing ever so noticeably over the years to hint at her true age, which Emma guessed to be close to seventy.

Emma flopped down on the chair, which was still warm from Marjorie's body heat. She waited for the phone to start ringing, but not a single call came in. She was already bored. She could start her homework or...she could text Holly. Just to say hi. And to ask how things were going. Things like Jackson maybe.

"Why is nothing right? Why?" Isaac Muñoz leaned over the side counter of the desk, waving several sheets of paper. "I need the originals of these purchase orders. Nothing is matching up. Nothing! The Chantilly lace is in the Shetland lace box.

"Where's Marjorie?" Isaac demanded when he finally noticed Emma, not Marjorie, sitting behind the desk. He was wearing tight jeans and an even tighter white tee.

"In search of decent-tasting caffeine," Emma explained calmly. Emma was used to Isaac's hysterics. The warehouse manager only operated at one speed: overdrive. Ever since her dad had laid off staff and Isaac had had to do two or three other jobs on top of his original duties, he had been even more tightly wound than usual. But Isaac somehow managed to keep Laceland chugging along—almost single-handedly—so everyone just sort of dealt with his freak-outs.

"Well, I need help. Now. You're drafted. Let's go, Rose Junior."

Emma pressed a button to forward the office phone directly to voice mail and followed Isaac back toward the freight elevator.

"Isaac!" Emma gasped. "There must be a million boxes of lace here!"

"Unloading boxes is good for your health," Isaac said.

"Makes you strong." He rested his portable speaker on the windowsill and pressed play. The deep voice of a guy rapping in both Spanish and English against a funky electronic backbeat filled the air.

With long, smooth movements, Isaac ran his X-Acto knife along the tape seams on the first box—lengthwise and then crosswise—and then moved on to the next one.

"Grab the packing lists, and check to make sure everything we ordered is inside," he instructed.

Emma redid the elastic on her ponytail and pulled the sheet of paper from the box. "First up, *amigo*, organza lace."

Two hours and twenty-five boxes of lace later, Emma wound her way toward the back of the warehouse and around some tall filing cabinets her dad had used to create a wall. She slipped into her favorite place. Her design studio.

Okay, maybe it wasn't exactly as fancy as the word "studio" made it sound, but it was totally her space, and she loved it. A thrill ran up her spine every time she walked in. She turned on the huge industrial light above her high, extra-wide metal worktable, illuminating a half-dozen vintage cookie tins full of her tiny treasures—fabric flower pins, crushed velvet ribbons, metallic sequins, and buttons in every color of the rainbow in all different shapes she'd been collecting since she was a little girl—along with her beloved Faber Castell colored-pencil set and a small stack of new unlined sketch pads bound in colorful fabrics that she picked up all over the city, from quirky little shops in Chinatown to art-supply stores.

Her eight-foot-high inspiration wall towered above the other side of the table. It was a much bigger version of the inside of her locker at school. The wall was plastered with magazine clippings—outrageously out-there editorial fashion spreads; printouts of her favorite pieces from the fashion shows in New York, Paris, Milan, and London that she had seen online; swatches of fabrics; sketches of designs she planned to make; and on-the-go snapshots of street fashion.

Off to the side sat her most prized possession—an old Singer sewing machine. For Emma's fourteenth birthday last spring, Grandma Grace, who had taught Emma everything she knew about sewing, surprised Emma by giving her granddaughter her beloved machine. It was still in its original console, which Emma loved because it meant the base of the sewing machine was flush with the table it sat in, giving her a flat surface to sew on. The Singer was so much better than the eBay bargain machine she'd been using for years. Emma promised to take good care of it and use it often.

She perched on the rickety wood stool and looked next to the table at the three dress forms she had been lucky enough to salvage on 37th Street over the past few months. It would've taken her years to save up to buy just one new dress form since they cost five hundred dollars or more.

Right now, all three were modeling dresses Emma had made with the juiciest accordion silk fabric she'd stumbled onto at a tiny Indian import shop on 36th Street. The colors had been so intense they practically screamed at her from the window, even though they were just draped in a heap over a folding chair. She bought bolts of deep, ripe raspberry; a rich pineapple yellow; and a tangy mango orange.

For the dresses, she had kept the lines simple with flirty, uneven skirts that dipped and rose in different places. A halter top for the raspberry, a racer-back tank for the orange one. And she'd done a simple boat-neck tank for the yellow. She'd made wonderful, whimsical sashes out of the silk fabric scraps, woven together and tied in a casual way that made them look like flower petals.

Emma stood and circled the dresses, eyeing them from various angles. She loved the way even the horrible fluorescent overhead light shimmered on the fabric. The halter and racer-back tops were great. But the boat neck felt a bit too tailored for the fabric. Emma picked up a tiny remnant of the orange accordion silk and twisted it into a flower. She held it around the neckline and then pinched the right shoulder of the dress, making

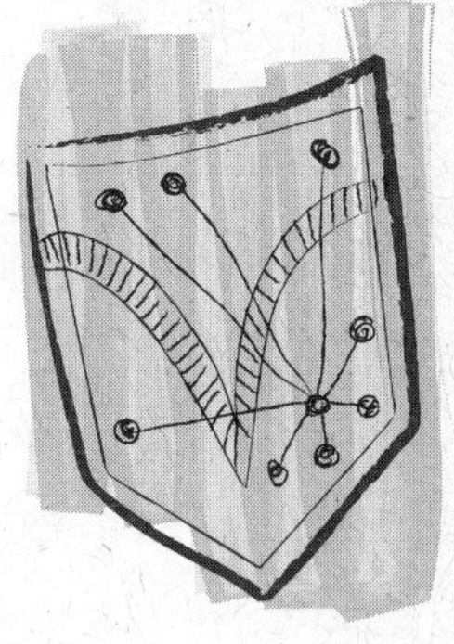

it just a bit asymmetrical. She pinned the flower onto the gathered shoulder and stood back to examine the new line of it and the little spray of orange against the yellow.

She tried to imagine how the dress would look when worn by someone—someone on a date, someone celebrating a happy occasion, someone confident and worldly. How would the dress look moving? Dancing? Twirling?

When Emma finally hung a finished piece on the rolling rack against the back wall, it was no longer simply an item of clothing. It was the beginning of a story that would unfold when someone put it on for the very first time. A story that would change and grow each time the piece was worn. Oh the secrets, she thought, that clothes could tell!

"That's potent," a guy's voice said from behind her.

Such a Charlie Calhoun word—*potent.* Emma turned and caught her friend eyeing her latest creation with almost as much attention as she gave her own work. "Do you really like it?"

"Do I ever say anything I don't mean?" Charlie didn't wait for an answer. "I like the shape and the material. Those colors look really cool together. I like how the yellow one is uneven. Makes it edgier."

Emma couldn't help but smile. She knew Charlie was always totally honest with her—for better or worse. He never played down his opinions, which she appreciated even when the Truth According to Charlie may not have been exactly what she wanted to hear or when she wanted to hear it.

At Amber Vigeant's twelfth birthday party, Charlie had told Emma—right in front of cute Mike Sheehan—that Emma had something gross hanging out of her nose. Beyond mortifying. And yes, Mike's laughter, as she ran to find a tissue, rang in her ears for weeks, but Emma reasoned it was better than spending the night talking to Mike with boogers on display.

Not all kids at Downtown Day shared her view about Charlie's truth-telling. A lot of people thought Charlie was rude. But Holly and Emma liked that he was so bold. They usually found it funny.

"What are you doing here?" Emma asked, as if she didn't already know.

"I don't feel like going home yet." Charlie was her only friend who ever visited her at Laceland. He actually liked it there, more than being at home with his kind of crazy mom who gave acting lessons in their tiny apartment when she wasn't auditioning for parts in Broadway shows. Holly kept promising to come by but never did. Emma was beginning to realize a lace warehouse didn't hold the same allure as shopping or seeing a movie with Ivana. Or being in the park with cute boys.

Charlie pushed his blue-tinted sunglasses up onto his white-blond hair. He showed up in a new pair of shades every day—each one cooler than the last. He reached for the bolt of blackwatch plaid fabric on the table. "Making kilts next?"

Emma shrugged. "Doubtful, but you never know. It was on the bargain rack at Allure Fabrics. You wouldn't wear a kilt if I made you one, would you?"

Charlie wiggled his blond eyebrows. "I might. I do have awesome legs."

She laughed. "I bet you do."

"Emma." Her dad peered around the file-cabinet blockade and nodded in Charlie's direction. He was as used to Charlie being around the warehouse as Emma was. "Charlie, I need to pull Emma away. She's got to earn some of that money I'm paying her."

"You can't be serious," Emma protested. "I have *definitely* earned every penny today! I just spent two hours unpacking boxes with Isaac. And I have the lace lint all over me to prove it!"

"True," her father agreed, leaning his elbow on top of one of the filing cabinets. It was kind of funny that her dad sold delicate lace—people were always shocked by that when they first met him. He was so tall and broad that he looked like he belonged on a football field.

"But, Cookie," Noah said, using the nickname he had called Emma since before she could hold a pencil in her hand, "you'll like this. Customers." His green eyes twinkled.

"Really? People? We never get people," Emma joked, though she had to admit her curiosity was definitely piqued. For the most part, no one needed to come to Laceland. Her dad had sales reps who traveled to manufacturing companies, selling them the lace they used to trim thousands of identical dresses and tablecloths and whatnots.

"I'll hang here," Charlie offered, his iPod headphones already in his ears.

Emma followed Noah down the hall. "Who's the customer?"

"You'll have to see for yourself. You're in for quite a surprise."

SO TAHITIAN SUNSET

Emma entered the well-lit but rarely used showroom, and her eyes immediately fixated on the unrolled bolt of lace on the glass display table. A light shone up from under the table, illuminating the exquisite petal-thin white design. The floral pattern was extremely detailed. This lace was gorgeous, so much nicer than any of the lace they usually had in the warehouse. *It must be a special order,* Emma thought, totally intrigued. *It looks handmade and crazy expensive.*

"It's so pretty!" Emma exclaimed, before realizing that there were two people in the room with their heads bent over the other side of the table.

"It is, isn't it? I told you to trust me, Paige. People will melt with envy when they see your dress. Complete and total meltdown," gushed a short woman with caramel-colored skin, cropped black hair that grazed her jawline at a sharp angle, and cat's-eye glasses. She wore a twill trench coat with silver metallic threads shot through it to give the material a subtle sheen. The nontraditional fabric was Emma's tip-off that the coat must be a designer piece. She couldn't help but wonder who had made it.

The cat's-eye-glasses woman nodded encouragingly at the woman circling the display table, who was intently analyzing the lace from every angle. That woman, Paige, was also striking but in a very different way. Tall and elegant, with peachy-pink skin and long, black hair twisted and pinned up in that perfect-yet-messy style that Emma could never get quite right with her hair even after a zillion tries.

Paige bit her glossed mauve lip and finally let out a breath. "It's good. The bodice will be amazing in this lace, right?"

The petite woman nodded furiously. "One hundred percent. By the time I'm done with it, it'll be perfect. To-die-for gorgeous. They'll be tripping all over themselves to get a photograph of you in this dress."

Paige smiled slightly. "I just have to

see it all myself. To be sure," she explained to Emma and her dad.

"Of course," Noah agreed. "It's your wedding. Most important dress of your life."

"Everyone thinks I've become a whacked-out, micro-managing bridezilla—even more of a perfectionist than usual, which is all very possible," Paige confessed, smoothing the front of her slim-cut, gray knit minidress, which Emma thought was gasp-worthy. "But they'll be positively vicious when I walk down the aisle. Everyone will want to find something wrong with my dress. You know they will, Lara."

"They'll have to look elsewhere," said the smaller woman, whom Emma now realized must be Paige's wedding dress designer. "Your choices are spectacular. They always are."

"If they weren't, *Madison* wouldn't be *the* fashion bible, now would it?" Noah said, grinning warmly.

Wait...what did Dad just say? Emma wondered. Why did he just bring up Madison? It had always been Emma's favorite fashion magazine, because it was the only one that truly focused on designers and their clothes. No silly articles about preventing wrinkles and choosing vacation spots or throwing flawless dinner parties. Noah knew that his designing daughter totally loved *Madison*.

"Oh, I'm late," Paige suddenly announced, as her eyes

darted to the wall clock above Noah's head. "I've got to get back to the office. If anyone there knew I snuck out on personal business..." She grimaced, crossed her eyes, and made a slashing-of-her-neck motion with her forefinger. "Lara, can you figure out how they should get the lace to you? I desperately need to find a ladies' room before I leave. It could take forever to get a cab at this hour."

"I'll take care of that with Ms. Suarte," Noah said. "This is Emma. She'll show you where to go, Ms. Young."

Oh. My. God! Paige is *Paige Young?* She is the senior fashion editor at *Madison!* This was *big*. It was like a rock star appearing at a school chorus rehearsal. Or the President of the United States showing up at a student council meeting. And on top of that, Paige Young's dress designer was Lara Suarte.

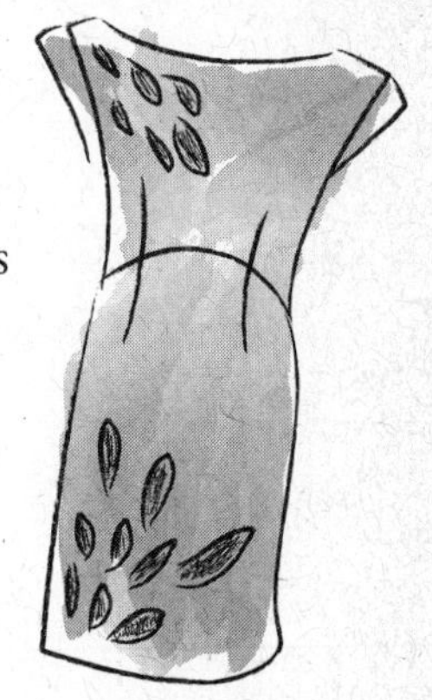

Emma remembered reading an article in *Madison* about her. She had recently become the go-to wedding-dress designer for Hollywood celebrities. So not only was Emma in the presence of a *real* fashion designer for the very first time, but also she was about to lead one of the most influential up-and-coming fashion editors to the bathroom!

"You okay, Em?" Noah asked, putting his large paw-hand on her shoulder.

"I kind of have to go now, if you don't mind," Paige pleaded, shifting from one slender stiletto heel to the other. "I just had a ginormous latte."

"S-sure," Emma stammered. She gestured for the fashion editor to follow her down Laceland's long narrow hall to the bathroom, which was at the far end of the warehouse.

The two walked in silence. The only sound was Paige's heels clicking on the bare wooden floors. Emma could barely speak, so she pointed at the ladies' room door and turned on the light for her, since the switch was inconveniently located outside the bathroom behind some shelves. Paige waved her thanks and shut the door behind her.

Emma leaned against the wall to wait. She hadn't said more than two words since Paige arrived. How can I get Paige to remember me? Emma wondered. I need to find something semi-intelligent to say before she's gone, so I can make some kind of impression—as something other than the lint-covered girl who once walked her to the bathroom. But what?

Emma knew that Paige Young could make or break a fashion career. And even though Emma had many years of school and training ahead of her, Paige could be editor-in-chief of *Madison* by the time she was ready to show her designs. She couldn't let this moment pass her by. If only her brain would start working...

They walked back to the showroom in silence. Emma felt her once-in-a-lifetime opportunity evaporating with every click of Paige Young's stilettos. She ran through and rejected possibilities.

I design clothes. Who cares?

I want to be a fashion designer when I grow up. Could I sound any more like a pre-couture five-year-old?

I love clothes. Duh. Who doesn't?

As they reached the reception area, Emma turned in an attempt to form words. She figured even a lame "nice meeting you" was better than being mute-girl. But Paige wasn't there. She wasn't anywhere!

Oh, no, Emma thought. I lost the fashion editor!

Emma raced back down the hall and into the dim warehouse. She retraced her steps to the bathroom, but Paige was nowhere to be found. Emma looked over toward her work space. It was the only area in the back of the warehouse that was lit up. Could Paige have thought that's where the showroom was? Emma wondered. She hurried around the filing-cabinet wall. There was Paige! Emma breathed a sigh of relief.

Until she saw her standing by the three dress forms and staring at Emma's three sorbet-colored dresses.

Paige reached out and touched the fabric of each dress with a light, practiced touch.

Emma's heart began to pound so loudly she was almost positive that Paige could hear it. Charlie looked up and took off his headphones. Emma shot him a "please-keep-quiet" look. By some miracle, he seemed to get the message.

"Love!" Paige exclaimed. "They're so...Tahitian Sunset!"

Had Paige Young just used the word "love" about Emma's dresses?

Before Emma knew what was happening, Paige whipped out her digital camera from her oversized black leather bag and started snapping away.

"Who designed these dresses?" Paige asked without turning around.

Uh-oh. Now what? Emma couldn't tell her *she* was the designer. Paige would probably laugh, or worse, pat Emma on the head and give her some lukewarm encouragement. And Paige clearly was up on all the latest work by real designers—after all, that was her *job*—so if Emma told her the dresses were made by someone famous she would most likely know Emma was lying. Besides, how would Emma explain why these pieces were in the back corner of this random lace warehouse?

Just as suddenly as it had started, Paige's photo frenzy stopped. She faced Emma and put her hands on her hips. "I know you can speak. I heard you before."

I've got to say something, Emma thought frantically. She racked her brain for an idea. She hadn't been this nervous since the time she had to give her first viola recital. She hated viola and hated having to play it in front of people even more. Her Italian music teacher kept whispering, "Play allegra! *Allegra!*" An instruction Emma never understood. The word sounded more like a pretty girl's name than a way to play the string instrument of torture.

"Allegra."

"Allegra—?" Paige asked.

Had she said it out loud? Now she couldn't take it back! Her comatose brain was suddenly in sugar-rush mode. *It wasn't bad,* she thought. *Allegra.* Some of the greatest fashion designers are Italian. *Allegra* works. I need a last name. A last name that also sounds Italian. *Dolce, Gabbana, Pucci, Armani*—every name that swirled through her fashion-obsessed mind was already taken. Her eyes desperately roamed her studio for inspiration, landing on a pretty red and white tin box that now housed her straight pins but had once held biscotti, a holiday gift sent by one of her dad's customers.

"Allegra Biscotti!" Emma blurted. Emma could see Charlie's eyes widen, but thankfully he didn't laugh or snort or even blink.

"Allegra Biscotti," Paige repeated slowly. "Is she around?"

She believes me! Emma thought, wide-eyed. "Uh, no, sorry. She's not here right now. And I'm pretty sure she's gone for the day," Emma said, using her best answering-the-office-phones voice that Marjorie had taught her.

Paige pursed her lips and turned back to the dress forms. She reached out and touched the raspberry dress again, feeling the fabric between her thumb and forefinger. "Do you know if this one is for sale?"

"Yes, it is!" Charlie piped in.

Emma shot Charlie an *I'm-gonna-kill-you!* look behind Paige's back. But he just waved his hand a few times. Go with it!

"Are you sure?" Paige asked, turning back to Emma.

"I am," Emma said, trying to unclench her teeth and speak normally. "Because, um, Allegra sometimes sells directly to private customers and we, uh, help her do that," she attempted.

Paige seemed to buy that, too, because she said, "Well,

the raspberry one is just *bananas*, it's so good. I have to have it. I need to get in touch with Ms. Biscotti ASAP. How do I do that?"

That was a really good question. How *did* someone get in touch with a fake fashion designer who was actually a fourteen-year-old girl standing right there?

Paige's cell phone trilled from deep within her oversized bag. "Got to pause," she said to Emma as she dug for her phone and walked a few steps away to take the call.

Emma was about to ask Charlie what she should do, but Paige returned much faster than she expected.

"Now I *really* have to bolt. Major crisis," she explained. "One of the rock stars we were shooting for our music issue borrowed the Chloe dress we photographed her in for a red-carpet event last night. She promised-promised-promised she'd return it by the end of today. *Naturellement*, she didn't bring it back, and she's leaving tonight to start her tour in Tokyo. Which means I have to go wrangle it back so I don't get in trouble with the designer, who loaned it to us in the first place. Craziness, right? I swear, there is *never* a dull moment," she said shaking her head. "So, about that contact info...?"

"*Right!* Right. I'll write it down for you." Emma plucked a scrap of paper off her worktable and signaled Charlie to hand her his pen. Heart racing, she scribbled down some numbers.

"Thanks!" Paige grabbed the piece of paper without looking at it. "That way out, right? I think I can find it. And please don't forget to ask Ms. Biscotti about the dress. I happen to be a perfect size four, so it shouldn't need any alterations. *Ciao* for now!"

Emma waited until she couldn't hear the clack-clack of Paige's footsteps anymore to finally let out her breath—which she suddenly realized she had been holding for most of the past five minutes. "Wow! I think I just made my very first sale—and to a major fashion editor! That really happened, right? You saw the same thing I did, didn't you, Charlie? I didn't just imagine it—?"

But Charlie was doubled over in laughter.

"Charlie! What? Why are you laughing? Was this some sort of prank?"

"No!" Charlie inhaled deeply to catch his breath. "No...I just want to...know...*how* you came up...with the name 'Allegra Biscotti'!"

"I'm not sure. It kind of came out of nowhere. Besides, what's wrong with Allegra Biscotti? I mean, other than the fact she doesn't exist." Emma crossed her arms over her chest.

"Nothing! It's great." Charlie still laughed.

Emma laughed, too. It was kind of funny. Crazy, really.

"And now you have your very first customer," Charlie pointed out. "Well, *Allegra's* very first customer but still. Awesome." Suddenly, Charlie turned serious. "Wait. What phone number did you give her?"

"My cell. Is that bad? I didn't know what else to do," Emma explained.

"Bold choice," he said. "But it sounds like she's actually going to call you—I mean, call Allegra—to find out about that dress."

"Oh, no!" Emma cringed. So not-smart. "When she calls that number, she's going to hear Holly and me scream-singing a Black Eyed Peas song on my outgoing message."

Charlie tossed Emma her cell phone from the table. "I'm thinking you might want to change that back to the generic greeting, *Allegra*."

SMOKIN' HOT NEW DESIGN TALENT

"Emma! Are you up yet? And by 'up' I mean actually out of bed!" her mother shouted from down the narrow hall of the Roses' apartment.

"Yes!" Emma stared into the organized chaos of her tiny closet. Though it was no wider than the length of her arm, it held an impressive number of clothes and accessories. Emma used antique hooks scavenged at flea markets, stacked sweater boxes decorated with collages she made from magazines, and a few extra shelves her dad had built to keep her closet tidy.

Maybe I'll wear that smoky-purple silk scarf I picked up on the street near school, Emma thought. One of the best things about Downtown Day was that the exclusive private school was located in SoHo, one of Emma's favorite neighborhoods. It had tons of cool boutiques and art galleries. Just peeking in the windows gave her inspiration for her designs. She stood on tiptoe, reached up, and slid out a box that she had decoupaged with cutouts of colorful flowers.

"What did you say?" her mother called, her voice sounding closer now.

Emma rolled her eyes, plucked out the scarf, and slid the box back into place. She swung open her bedroom door. It wasn't like her family's three-bedroom apartment was so huge that her mother couldn't hear her behind the closed door. But Emma knew this was one of her mother's tricks to make sure her kids weren't still in bed. "I'm up! Satisfied?"

"Very," her mother said. "You know how I love torturing you and your brother every morning. It's my favorite part of the day."

"I thought bugging us about homework was your favorite part," Emma mumbled.

"I'm ignoring that." Her mother rapped on William's door. "Will! Up! Now!"

Emma gently shut her door. Normally, she would still be lying in bed, trying to squeeze in a few more minutes of sleep. She knew her mother woke them up earlier than really necessary, scared they would make her late for work. Mom taught English and composition—at Emma's school. When she first started Downtown Day, Emma was really proud of the fact. She used to visit her mother's classroom all the time and beg to help grade papers.

Now, she rerouted through the halls with the primary mission of avoiding her mother. Sure, Joan Rose taught in the high school, which was attached to the middle school, but that was really just a technicality. Any way she looked at it, Emma went to school with her mother. Way too much family-togetherness time.

But this morning, the excitement of meeting Paige Young was still so fresh in her mind that the minute Emma opened her eyes, she jumped out of bed. What happened yesterday at Laceland was too mind-blowing for words. She didn't even care if anything ever came of it. Emma switched on her laptop. She hoped Holly was online so she could tell her all about Paige. Holly had been missing in action all night.

As the computer started up, Emma went back to her closet. What can I wear with the scarf? she wondered. Maybe those narrow khaki riding pants with the brown suede patches on the inner knees she'd bought on a whim last spring. She reached for the pants and held them up with the scarf, considering the combo. Good, but she'd have to find a top and shoes that were the complete opposite of horsey. She definitely didn't want to look like she was dressing for Halloween.

Emma glanced at the computer screen. Neither Holly nor Charlie was logged on. Figured. She clicked open her favorite bookmarks and rolled the cursor over the link to StylePaige .com, Paige Young's own blog. Emma had just looked at it last night, but she felt like reading it again. It made yesterday more real. She needed to spend a few more minutes reliving it all before the reality of school crashed down around her.

The home page featured the usual stuff—reviews of fashion shows, the latest "it" bag for fall, and some young, starved model who was the hot, new runway sensation. Emma stared at the artfully photographed picture of Paige Young at the top of the right column. She clicked "Refresh" and then scrolled down the page for another few seconds. The clock at the bottom of the screen said 7:02...oops, 7:03. She had to get moving. Just as she turned away, something caught her eye. She whirled back around. A new posting.

Emma gasped. Leaning closer, nose almost touching the screen, she read the latest headline out loud, "Smokin' Hot New Design Talent Discovered Yesterday: Exclusive First Peek at Allegra Biscotti!"

Emma blinked really hard and looked at the page again. There it was: Allegra Biscotti.

That's me! Emma thought. I'm on StylePaige!

There were photos—photos of *her* dresses! She couldn't stop staring. They looked so good. So professional. So *real.*

Emma noticed a short paragraph under the headline. She sank into her desk chair and began to read:

Deep in the heart of the Garment District, Allegra Biscotti has been quietly working away on three of the freshest designs I've seen in *eons*. (See my exclusive pix below!) Helped by the yummy sorbet colors, these playful and imaginative dresses hit just the right note, like the first truly warm day of the season. One thing's for sure: this style spotter is going to have her eyes peeled for more from Allegra Biscotti!

Emma leaped up and whirled around her room. She didn't know what to do first. She wanted to cheer, to dance, to celebrate with someone! She swung open her door and ran out into the hallway. Her mother's angry voice from the kitchen stopped Emma in her tracks.

"William! Are you kidding me with this? You are *not* wearing basketball shorts to school!" her mother yelled. "Go change. *Now.*"

Emma tiptoed backward into her room and quietly closed the door. Nope, she wasn't about to get in the middle of whatever was going on out there. Charlie! She had to tell Charlie the good news. She grabbed her cell phone out of her school bag and hit the speed-dial.

"Whaaat?" Charlie whined after the second ring.

"Did I wake you?"

"Obviously," Charlie grumbled. "This better be good."

"It is, I promise!" The words tumbled out as she told him about the blog post on StylePaige. "And she even says at the end that she's 'going to have her eyes peeled for more from Allegra Biscotti!' How cool is that?"

"That so rocks!" Despite the remnants of sleep in his voice, Charlie sounded truly excited. "You're famous. Or Allegra is."

Emma couldn't stop grinning. "You know what's kind of weird, but in a good way? I'm reading about myself but not, you know? Right now, you and I are only two people on the planet who know that Allegra Biscotti is really me! I can't wait to tell Holly." She clicked on "Print" so she could take a copy of the posting with her to school.

Charlie yawned. "Can I go back to sleep now?"

"Sure, but don't you have to get up in like five minutes anyway?"

"Every minute counts."

Emma tapped her fingers against the metal door of her locker, her eyes trained on the end of the hall. She felt like she'd been waiting forever for Holly. She flipped open her phone to check the time—again. Less than ten minutes before the last bell. She was literally going to explode if she didn't get to tell Holly about Allegra.

The corridor became more crowded by the minute. Now she couldn't see the top of the stairs. Standing on tiptoe, she craned her neck to peer above her classmates' heads. Where could Holly be?

Suddenly, her eyes locked with Jackson Creedon's.

For a split second, the chaos of the students filling the hall dropped away. His eyes were so blue, his gaze so steady. What am I doing? Emma thought. He's going to think I'm staring at him! She ducked for cover behind Coco and pretended to organize her books. Had Jackson asked about her? Holly better show up soon!

Leaning back ever so slightly, Emma snuck another look at Jackson. She couldn't help it. After three weeks of being in the same few classes with him, she still didn't know much about him other than what she could observe from brief glances—okay, fine, when she *stared*—at him:

1. He was super-cute (obvious).
2. He was quiet (or at least not as loud as the guys he hung out with).
3. He spent a lot of time writing or drawing or doodling in his notebook, which made him seem like he was not paying attention in class, kind of like Emma, now that she thought about it. She so wished she could get her hands on that notebook...Yeah, like that was ever going to happen.
4. When he did look up at the teacher or the board, he had the cutest way of squinting and biting the right corner

of his bottom lip. She couldn't let herself look at the whole lip-biting thing for too long because it made her stomach spin...but in a good way.

The only other thing she knew about Jackson was that he played on Downtown Day's soccer team—not that she had ever been to a school soccer game before. Maybe I should go one of these days, Emma suddenly thought. Then I can stare at him freely. In fact, she reasoned, if I went to a soccer game and *didn't* watch, it would be rude.

In Emma's mind, Fantasy Jackson was deep and super-thoughtful. She imagined that he sometimes felt like he didn't fit in, even though he so clearly did. And after seeing him put a few pieces of scrap paper in the paper-recycling bin before leaving the classroom once during the first week of school, she imagined that he was super-caring about the planet.

In the Real World, a massively huge ocean separated them socially. He was in the cool crowd, and Emma was... not. Even though she had been going to school with most of these kids since the fourth grade, Jackson had been able to walk into school and immediately fit into the most popular crowd.

Then again, Emma hadn't ever *tried* to get into the popular crowd—not like Holly seemed to be doing now for some reason. Emma had realized that the only hope she had of getting to know Jackson was through the new Holly-Ivana alliance. At least that was a teeny, tiny ray of hope...because otherwise, there would have been no chance of their worlds ever crossing beyond the few classes they were both in.

There was a major downside to this social bridge to Jackson. Ivana came with Lexie, who so obviously wanted to be Jackson's girlfriend. Emma had seen Lexie purposely sit next to Jackson in biology on the first day of school, so she would wind up being his lab partner. And even though Lexie's locker was on a different corridor, Emma noticed that Lexie was always hanging out at Kayla's and Shannon's lockers, which were much closer to Jackson's.

It *was* within the realm of possibility, Emma supposed, that that particular piece of evidence could have less to do with Lexie being after Jackson and more to do with the Ivana-Bees' inability to be separated for more than thirty seconds at a stretch, but Emma highly doubted it.

After years of being in the same small school together, Emma knew that Lexie wasn't the type of girl who ever lost at anything. She got straight A's; she was the captain of the middle-school field-hockey team, which was undefeated last year; and most importantly, every semester since sixth grade, Lexie had decided who was going to be her boyfriend, and within a few weeks, she and the guy were a couple.

Not that Emma would ever admit it to anyone, but sometimes she envied Lexie's focus, drive, and determination. Lexie saw what she wanted and went after it. As Emma's brother, William, always said, probably parroting his favorite sportscaster, "You gotta be in it to win it." Lexie was *definitely* in it. Emma? Not so much.

"Earth to Emma!" Holly was suddenly standing next to Emma and waving her hands in front of her face.

"It took you long enough to get here!" Emma exclaimed. "We only have like two seconds before the next bell. Tell me everything that happened at the park yesterday. What did you find out?"

"Well," Holly began, clearly happy to dish. "Let's see. Jackson was there, of course. Looking very cute. Not that I thought so exactly, but you probably would. And he talked a lot more than usual. He was actually kind of funny, but you had to be paying attention or you wouldn't really notice."

I knew it! Emma thought. "What else?" She desperately wanted more detail so she could begin replacing Fantasy Jackson with Real Jackson.

"He was telling us about how he goes off to some crazy place in New Jersey on the weekends to ride dirt bikes with his cousins."

"Wow, that's pretty cool," Emma said, digesting this new tidbit. Suddenly Real Jackson and Fantasy Jackson melded as she pictured him wearing a black leather motocross jacket with red and white padded stripes on the elbows and shoulders, ripped jeans covered in mud, and heavy black motorcycle boots with silver rings on the ankles.

She could see them hanging out together, her wearing, of course, a matching leather jacket with brass studs, a black lace top, and a white gauzy skirt with lots of stiff crinoline underneath to give it that fun pouf—very rocker chick meets third-grade ballet recital. Emma's fashion reverie was interrupted by the grating sound of Ivana's voice.

"And the manicurist at the spa wouldn't stop calling me 'Wanda!' Can you believe it? I'm like, lady, the name's *I-va-na!*" The Ivana-Bees, flanking their leader, shrieked with laughter. Emma didn't think Ivana's story sounded that funny, but maybe

"you had to be there," as they said about practically every one of their experiences.

The three 'Bees paused as Ivana reached out to link her elbow with Holly's. "Holls, you coming with?" Ivana asked.

Emma cringed. Ivana had taken her nickname for Holly. Emma had been calling Holly that since the second grade, when they saw a movie about four best friends who made up nicknames for each other. It had sounded like a very mature and cool thing to do back then.

"Totally!" Holly slammed her locker door shut and slid into formation with the 'Bees. "Ivana, I love-love your sweater. It's awesome."

"I know, isn't it?" Ivana answered.

Emma eyed the sleeveless sweater—an obviously expensive cashmere with a small ruffle along the deep V-neckline. The color was just the right shade of lavender to set off Ivana's red, perfectly flat-ironed hair. Emma had seen the sweater in the window of Shape, the pricey SoHo boutique near school that provided Ivana with most of her wardrobe. Ivana wore it with the same ivory lacy camisole displayed on the mannequin. There are so many other fun ways she could've worn that, Emma thought, layering it in her mind with patterned sweaters and tops.

"Shaye," Holly continued, "did you do something different with your hair—part it on a different side, maybe? I like it. You should totally wear it that way all the time."

Shannon, who was the most tomboyish of the group, probably because she was growing taller without getting curvier, reached up to touch her brown chin-length hair with a confused but pleased look on her face. "I don't think so, but thanks!"

Holly turned to Kayla. "That lip gloss is killer, Kay. New?"

Kayla was like a walking advertisement for Beautylicious, the beauty company her mother had started five years earlier. She bragged about her mother all the time, as if she were the Secretary of State bringing about world peace instead of a makeup artist turned businesswoman.

Unlike Shannon, Kayla had no problem in the natural curves department. Plus she had been wearing a full face of makeup religiously since the age of twelve, which Emma thought made Kayla look, at times, like she was spending too much time with the clowns at the circus.

Now Kayla puffed out her lips so everyone could see. "Yeah, my mom just brought it home yesterday. It's not even in the stores yet. It's called 'Fire Starter.'"

Holly turned back toward Emma. "Hurry up, Emma! We're going to be late."

"Trying!" Emma yanked on her bag. The strap was stuck on something inside her locker. By the time she freed it and closed the door, the group was already halfway down the hall.

Emma sighed and walked at a normal pace. She couldn't bring herself to chase after them. Besides, now that Ivana and the 'Bees had swallowed up Holly, Emma knew that she wouldn't be able to finish their conversation. Or tell Holly about Allegra Biscotti. I'll grab her at lunchtime to eat with me in the student lounge, Emma decided. She knew Holly would celebrate with her once she found out the big news.

Emma scooted into the classroom just as Mr. Whitmore was closing the door.

The crescendo from the lunchroom hit Emma long before she even walked in the door. The cafeteria, which was in the basement next to the gym, was the worst room in the school. The ceiling was low, and the cement floor was painted the ugliest green color Emma had ever seen.

Since there were no windows, the only light was from the industrial fluorescent bulbs overhead, which Emma thought made everyone look like they had the flu. On top of all that, the lunchroom perpetually smelled like grease, even though the PTA had voted fried food off the menu two years earlier.

Emma stood in the doorway and scanned the buzzing room until she spotted Holly paying the cashier. I need to grab her, Emma thought.

Holly smiled when she saw Emma coming toward her. "There you are. You brought your lunch today, right?"

Emma always packed a yogurt and chips. The mysterious ingredients and origins of the school lunches were too baffling to a girl who never got higher than a B in chemistry. She liked being able to identify her food. "Do you want to go to the loun—"

Holly cut her off, lifting her tray with one hand and grabbing Emma's elbow with the other.

Emma's heart sank as soon as she realized where they were headed. "Remind me again why we have to sit with Ivana and the 'Bees?" she asked.

"Because everything's different now that we're in eighth grade," Holly explained. "Plus it's more fun to hang out with Ivana and the girls than those random people we used to sit with. You have to admit, Em, those kids are kind of weird."

"Charlie isn't weird," Emma protested, yanking back on Holly's arm to stop her before they reached the table. "We always had fun with him. He's our *friend*."

Holly snapped her gum. "Charlie barely eats in the cafeteria anymore. He's always off in the student lounge listening to his iPod or looking at those weird Japanese comic books. Trust me. He hasn't even noticed that we're gone."

That was sort of true, actually. Charlie liked being a bit of a shadow, fading in and out without anyone noticing. Plus, he hated crowds. And the color green. But Emma suspected that this new lunch-table situation had more to do with Holly being flattered that Ivana had invited her—and probably not *both* of them—to sit at her table. For the past few weeks, Emma had been going along with Holly's new seating arrangement. She figured as long as she got to sit with Holly, maybe it would be all right.

But so far, it hadn't been that great.

"Come on, Em! I'm *starving*." Holly gave Emma's elbow another tug, coaxing her toward the table.

Reluctantly, Emma gave in. They barely had twenty minutes left to eat lunch and would have even less by the time they got upstairs to the student lounge anyway. As Holly slid into the empty chair next to Ivana, Emma settled down in a seat at the end of table. The Ivâna-Bees were in the middle of a heated discussion about their ideas for this year's first fund-raiser.

"Last year, the eighth-grade class held a bake sale, and they raised a ton of money," Shannon said, nibbling on a carrot stick. The way she wrinkled her nose and scrunched up her face reminded Emma of a rabbit.

more IS more!

Ivana laughed loudly, tossing her long red hair over her shoulder as if she were in a shampoo commercial. "Shaye, you can't be serious. Remember the last time you tried to bake something? Di-SAS-ter!" Ivana turned to Holly. "She almost burned down her kitchen because she put the oven on broil instead of bake."

"The doorman had to come turn off the fire alarm because Shannon didn't know how to do it!" Kayla added—again just to Holly.

Holly giggled. "That's *hilarious*," she said. "I *so* wish I'd been there!"

Emma snuck a sideways glance at Holly to see if she was faking her enthusiasm. But Holly was totally serious.

"It was pretty embarrassing," Shannon admitted, though she seemed more flattered than embarrassed that she was the focus of attention. "But I still think a bake sale is a good idea."

"How about something that doesn't require using the oven—or any fire, for that matter?" Ivana suggested.

"I know! We could have a car wash!" Kayla leaned forward.

"*Ew!*" Lexie squealed. "I don't want to have to wash some weirdo-stranger's car!"

"Um, hello?" Ivana added. "We live in a city, remember? Most people don't even own cars."

Emma pretended to be fascinated with the last dollop of strawberry yogurt in the container. She swirled it around with her plastic spoon. Since she hadn't joined the Fund-Raising Committee like Holly and the other girls, she didn't have much to contribute. Nor had she signed up for the Social Committee or the Film Club, even though Holly had begged her to do those with her, too.

What was weird was that Emma and Holly had never been "joiners" before.

They had always been happy to move around the edges of all the groups without necessarily being a part of any one of them. Emma could tell who was who just by looking at what they wore. She had sketched them all, fascinated by how clothes ruled the cliques. Each group had their own style, she knew. If your clothes didn't fit in, than neither did you. For as long as they'd been friends, Emma and Holly had hung out with various kids from all of the groups, but they mostly spent their free time together because that's what they had the most fun doing.

Until this summer.

After school ended, Holly's workaholic parents had dragged her to their new weekend house in Litchfield, Connecticut. Holly complained to Emma via a torrent of daily text messages about how there was nothing to do and no one to do it with. But then Holly started to sound like she was having fun. That's when Ivana's name began popping up.

Ivana's mother and latest stepfather had a place in Litchfield, too. Emma was shocked. If she had been stranded on a desert island with Ivana, she would have sooner befriended a lizard than Ivana Abbott. When Emma complained about it to Charlie, he said that it was probably just a "friendship of convenience." Emma spent the rest of the summer hoping he was right.

But now it looked like he wasn't. Around the Ivana-Bees, Holly was different. Emma couldn't put her finger on how. She just knew that suddenly she felt like their friendship went from being the most natural, easiest thing in the world to requiring a conscious effort to keep it going.

"Maybe we could put on a fashion show," Holly said. "That'd be fun, wouldn't it, Em?"

Emma looked up, surprised. She had started to draw a new outfit for Ms. Ramirez, the dowdy cafeteria cashier, in her sketchbook. It was coming out like a futuristic jumpsuit. Maybe not the best look. "For what?"

"A class fund-raiser," Holly answered. "Don't you think we could build a catwalk in the gym and get some of the students and teachers to model? Maybe call some boutiques to see if they would let us borrow their clothes?"

Ivana and the 'Bees faced Emma expectantly.

"Um, I guess so," Emma answered.

"And you could be our fashion expert," Holly added enthusiastically.

Someone snickered, but Emma wasn't sure who. She glanced at the digital wall clock. Four minutes until lunch was over.

"*Or*," Ivana began, turning everyone's attention right back to her, "we could do an auction. I bet everyone's parents have something decent they could donate as prizes. It would be *so* much easier. My cousin is an event planner, and she always says how no one ever realizes how much work it is to do events. Plus they're super-expensive."

"An auction is such an amazing idea, Ivana!" Holly gushed, leaning forward in her chair.

Again, Emma was surprised by Holly's tone. Was Ivana's idea really that amazing? Hadn't auctions been done since the dawn of time—or at least, since the invention of school fund-raisers?

"Actually," Ivana continued, "I was thinking we could make it a green auction. You know, with all eco-friendly stuff."

"I bet my parents could score a free dinner at the organic restaurant they go to practically every Saturday night," Lexie said. "The restaurant's owners only use ingredients they can buy locally. That's green, right?"

"And my mom could donate a gift bag of her company's new all-natural makeup line," Kayla added proudly. "The stuff smells so good! I'll bring you samples. We have a ton at home."

And with that, the girls chattered on, excitedly throwing out ideas, each trying to top the other. Emma's momentary existence in their plans evaporated into the puke-green floor.

Emma slid the printout of the Allegra Biscotti post from Paige Young's blog from her sketchbook. Just looking at it made her heart jump. Her dresses! *Hers!*

Emma glanced at the clock again. The bell was just about to ring. Maybe she could get Holly to hang back for a few seconds while the other girls tossed their garbage. Then she could show Holly the blog and quickly tell her what happened with Paige…

"Holls, don't forget. We need to stop at your locker before class so you can give me your *To Kill a Mockingbird* notes from yesterday," Ivana said, already standing.

"Right!" Holly leaped up to follow Ivana. "See you later, Em."

Emma watched Holly and the girls leave the cafeteria. She wanted to stop Holly, but she suddenly felt glued to her seat, unable and unwilling to run after them. The noise level dropped as everyone headed for the halls. Emma continued to sit, gazing at the paper in the hands. *Allegra Biscotti.*

Not being able to tell Holly what happened with Paige didn't make it any less real. She knew that. She really did. And she didn't want to be upset—not now.

Someone important said I was a talented designer, and that's a really good thing, Emma reminded herself, finally standing to leave.

KILLER DRESS

Hey, watch it, buddy!" someone shouted at the man recklessly climbing up the crowded subway steps two by two and pushing people to the side—including Emma and her mom. After he disappeared, everyone grumbled but kept moving up and out onto the street before fanning in different directions. Just another morning in Manhattan.

Emma re-wrapped the sheer, crinkly, electric-blue gauzy scarf around her neck as she worked her way up the stairs. She had woken up feeling like a real fashion designer, and a sequin-sprinkled scarf was definitely in order. Her mother paused at the street corner to push her glasses back up her nose.

"It seems busier than usual today. Or maybe I shouldn't have had that second cup of coffee," she said. She eyed Emma. "Have you started studying for the Western civ test yet?"

It was the same question she'd asked last week. And Emma still had the same answer. Umm...no.

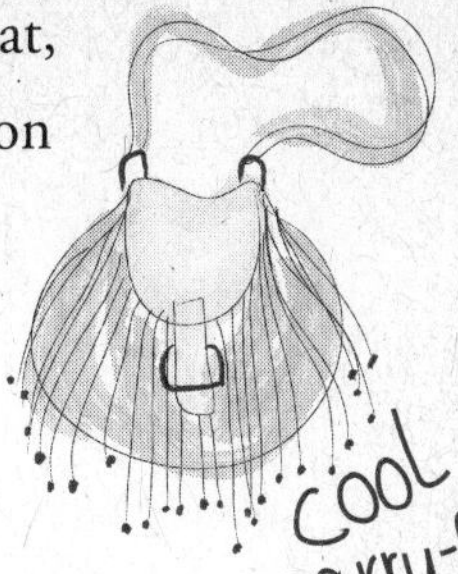

"Not yet," Emma replied, praying that, by some miracle, her mom would move on to some other subject. Any subject. But that was as likely as Prada selling their clothes at Marshalls.

"Why not?" her mom asked. She wanted Emma to take a hard test to get into an advanced Western civilization class that was only offered second semester and was taught by her mother's best friend, Betsy Ling. Studying for this test would be on top of the two or three hours of homework Emma already had every night.

"I've been pretty busy, especially at work." But Emma knew that her answer was not going to fly. Not with *her* mom, who acted like school was more important than everything, including breathing.

Her mother hiked her frayed, faded public-radio-station tote bag higher up on her shoulder. "I love that you're helping your dad at the warehouse after school, and it's great that you're continuing to practice your sewing after Grandma Grace spent all that time showing you how. But I don't want you to miss out on all the amazing academic opportunities you have, especially by being able to go to *this* school."

Practice? Emma cringed that her mom thought her

designing and sewing was some passing hobby. She thought about telling her about Allegra Biscotti but just as quickly changed her mind. Her mother would suck all the fun out of it. Plus this was about the one-billionth time she'd reminded Emma that she wouldn't even be attending Downtown Day if her mother wasn't teaching there. Going to a snooty private school for free was one of the few perks of being the daughter of a teacher. It was probably the only perk, Emma figured.

"Look," her mom continued, pushing the rectangular, green plastic-framed glasses that she had been wearing since the nineties back up her nose. "It's a small class, and Betsy has a really unique approach that I think you'd enjoy. It doesn't hurt to at least *try* getting in, does it?"

As Emma and her mother turned the corner, the sounds of kids in the enclosed school yard to the side of an eight-story, redbrick school building grew louder.

"It might hurt a little," Emma said, letting her fingers run along the chain-link fence, memorizing the diamond pattern to use later, possibly on the bodice of a dress. "It's not like I have tons of free time."

She wanted so badly to tell her mother that she didn't

want to take the test or the class. In her head, it sounded like a simple thing to say. But Emma couldn't get the words out. Probably because she already knew what her mother's answer would be. School first. Fashion second.

Her mother frowned. "Don't you have some free time at work? I doubt Dad has you working every single minute that you're there."

Emma felt her chest tighten. She spent her free time working on her designs. Her mother had never understood Emma's love of sketching, even though she'd been doing it since she was eight. And now that Emma was fourteen, the chances of her mother getting it seemed even smaller. Emma's education was the only thing her mom cared about. Clearly, she wasn't getting out of this. Her mother had won. Again. She would just have to find the time to study for the stupid test. Somehow.

"I'll start reviewing the study guide," Emma said. Just not today, she thought.

"Good." Emma could see her mother reviewing her mental to-do list: Nag daughter about schoolwork. Check. Just then, her mother's cell phone rang.

"It's Vice Principal Manning," her mother said, squinting at the caller ID. "I just have to speak to him for a sec. We can keep walking, though."

Emma pulled her own cell from her bag. Weird…it was

off. She pressed the power button, suddenly remembering that her mother had made her stop texting Charlie and shut it down to finally get serious about homework last night.

Coming back to life, the phone vibrated in her hand. Two new voice-mail messages and four missed calls from a number she didn't recognize. Someone had actually been looking for her in the night, and her phone had been off! What was going on? Who was it?

Emma touched her mother's arm to get her attention. "I just remembered. I need to go to the library before homeroom to look up something for world history."

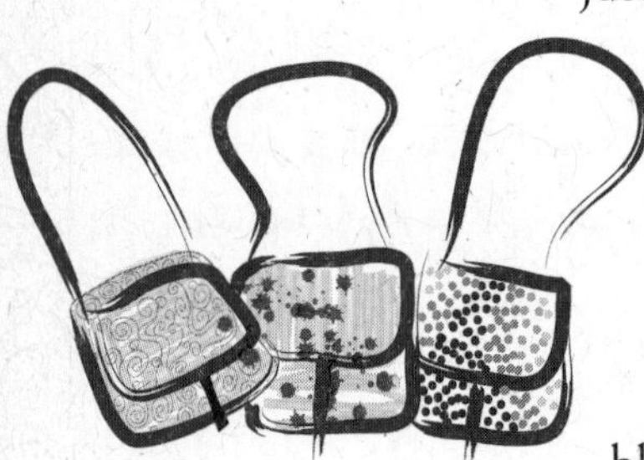

Her mother nodded and waved. Emma walked quickly down the block, her black canvas messenger bag—detailed with Klimt-like swirls she'd drawn on with metallic gel pens—swinging against her hip. She dialed into her voice mail.

"Hello, Ms. Biscotti. My name is Paige Young—" Emma's heart skipped a beat. Oh. My. God. It was *her*.

Emma glanced back, but her mother was out of sight. Ducking into the doorway of a closed restaurant, she started the message again.

"Hello, Ms. Biscotti. My name is Paige Young, and I'm

the senior fashion editor at *Madison* magazine. I just wanted to share with you what I hope you'll think is ah-mazing news. I recently posted a very positive piece about you and your to-die-for designs on my fashion blog, StylePaige.com, which I hope you caught. After seeing the item, my editor-in-chief at the magazine went ahead and picked up the posting for *Madison's* online edition. I hope you're thrilled! Thanks so much. Ciao."

Emma leaned back against the door of the restaurant, took a deep breath, and replayed the message. And then she played it one more time just to make sure she had heard it right. *Madison* magazine published the post about Allegra Biscotti on its website! *Amazing* was right! Then she remembered she had a second message. Hopefully, it wasn't Paige calling back to say that they'd changed their minds.

"Hi, Ms. Biscotti. It's Paige Young again. I'm sorry for the cell-phone stalking, but I wanted to make sure that the kids at Laceland gave you my message about purchasing your gasp-worthy, beautiful raspberry halter dress. I just about died when I saw it in your studio a few days ago. I have to have it and would love to get it before anyone else does! I hope it's not already spoken for. It would be perfect for my honeymoon…Anyway, when you get a chance, would you mind giving me a call so we can discuss further? Thanks so much! Ciao!"

Emma clutched the phone to her stomach and closed her eyes. *Madison* magazine's website. Paige Young wanting her dress. It's *really* happening, she told herself. I'm not imagining this. I have the messages to prove it!

Even so, she carefully saved both voice mails so she could replay them later for Charlie and Holly—and for herself—just to make sure she'd heard what Paige said correctly. It was a good thing Charlie had her change her personal greeting back to the generic one. Paige clearly believed that this was Allegra Biscotti's cell-phone number. From now on, Emma vowed to be extra careful not to answer her phone if a call came in from either of those numbers.

Filled with a surge of energy, she sprinted the rest of the way to school. She had to see the item about Allegra Biscotti on *Madison*'s website with her own eyes. Racing up the steps two at a time, her brain began to process Paige's call. How was she going to find a way for Allegra to call back Paige? And what about the dress Paige wanted?

Emma hoped Charlie would know what to do.

Sitting still during her morning classes was almost impossible, much less paying attention to anything her teachers said. Her silver sneaker tapped the linoleum floor impatiently. Waiting. Waiting. After what seemed like years, geometry class finally finished. She rushed to the library for study hall. She needed to get in front of a computer.

Emma knew she had to score a carrel that wasn't in full view of the librarian, cranky Ms. Williams. She pushed through the double swinging doors and instantly saw that all the good seats were taken. The one day I want to sneak a look at an outside site, and I can't, Emma thought in frustration.

Then she spotted Holly waving to her. Holly sat in the best carrel of all—the one farthest away from the librarian's desk and turned at just the right angle so Ms. Williams couldn't see the screen. Excellent! Emma hurried toward Holly, knowing the desk next to hers would work, too. And that's when Emma saw her.

Kayla. Sitting at the desk next to Holly's.

Holly didn't save me a seat, Emma realized. She was so surprised that she actually stopped moving. Just stood there and stared. It didn't make sense. They usually sat together, and whoever got there first would hold the spot next to her for the other.

Holly shrugged, gave a lame half-smile, and put up her hands as if to say, "Sorry."

Emma wandered like a lost child to an empty desk across the room.

Madison, she thought as she slid into the chair and shook

the mouse to bring the sleeping computer screen to life. Forget Holly. Think Allegra.

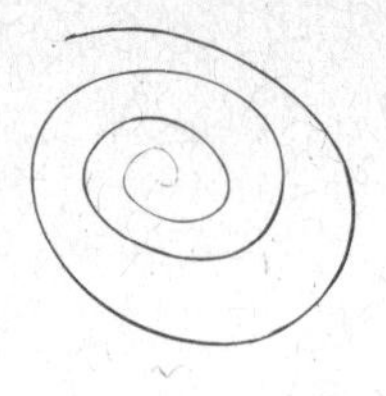

With the librarian's eagle eyes on her, Emma had no options. She pulled up the Western civ online study guide and tried to make her eyes focus on the words. Boring. If she couldn't get through the study guide, how was she going to make it through a whole class of this stuff next semester?

There was definitely no getting out of that test. Her mother wasn't about to let that happen. If Emma failed the whole thing completely, her mother would know she hadn't studied at all. That was the problem with being more than somewhat intelligent.

Emma watched Ms. Williams—who wore a frilly white blouse with a Peter Pan collar and a thin, fitted daffodil-colored cardigan sweater with tiny pearl buttons—for signs of movement. Emma always had trouble making the connection between the witchy librarian and her sweet-schoolgirl-from-the-1950s outfits. Which was the real Ms. Williams?

Ms. Williams stayed firmly planted in her seat. Is she going to sit at her desk forever just to torture me or what? Emma thought desperately. Please get up! Please, please, please get up!

As if motivated by the silent plea, Ms. Williams finally stood with a stack of books and DVDs and walked toward the rolling shelves. This was Emma's chance. She quickly typed the Web address for *Madison* magazine, her fingers hovering over the keyboard as she waited for the page to load. That seemed to take forever, but then there it was, with almost the same headline as on StylePaige: "Smokin' Hot New Design Talent Discovered by Our Own Paige Young: Exclusive First Peek at Allegra Biscotti!"

Even though Emma had known the post was going to be there, seeing it felt totally different. There it was, at the top of the page with the photos that Paige had taken. The paragraph was pretty much what Paige had written for her blog, but now it was on an official magazine website that was seen by hundreds of thousands of people, possibly as far away as Europe and Japan. Plus, on the same page as the item about Allegra Biscotti was news about many mega-famous designers—Marc Jacobs, Michael Kors, and Donna Karan. Allegra Biscotti, who hadn't even existed a few days ago, was suddenly sharing page space with some of the most successful designers in the world!

Emma clapped her hand over her mouth to stop herself from whooping out loud in the hushed library. She quickly minimized the page, as if everyone in the room would know that "Allegra Biscotti" was really Emma Rose. She looked around to make sure no one was paying attention to her. As usual, they weren't.

Emma clicked on the browser to reopen it. She leaned back in her chair and turned slightly. She wanted to get Holly's attention so she could show her the screen. But how? She couldn't say her name out loud. Ms. Williams would be all over her in two seconds flat. Not only did the librarian have eagle eyes, she also had elephant ears.

So Emma tried staring at Holly's back, hoping she'd feel Emma's eyes on her and turn around. But Holly was too busy IMing with Kayla to notice anything.

"Killer dress," a girl Emma only sort of knew whispered as she walked by, nodding at the screen on Emma's computer.

"I did that! Those are mine!" Emma screamed, though only in her mind. But right now, the only person she cared about telling was her best friend, even if she hadn't saved her a seat. If Holly would just look over at her...but Ms. Williams was now walking back toward her desk at the front of the room.

Emma reluctantly returned to the study guide. But even as she tried to absorb the answers to the sample test questions, all she could see were Allegra Biscotti's name and her designs gracing the pages—admittedly the digital pages—of *Madison* magazine.

"Can you do any impersonations? You know, someone with a heavy Italian accent?" Charlie asked later that afternoon as he dodged a rolling rack of clothes being pushed down the narrow sidewalk on Seventh Avenue. Emma was ready to explode by the time Charlie found her at her locker after school, and the two chatted nonstop for the entire walk to the 1/9 train and the ride uptown.

Every time Emma came up from the subway on 34th Street, a jolt of excitement shot though her. Emma loved the Garment District. It didn't matter that it was always so loud and dirty and crowded. It was the epicenter of the fashion business. It thrilled Emma to walk up Fashion Avenue, which was what Seventh Avenue had been renamed because so many famous clothing and accessories designers' studios were located there.

Not that she ever really saw any celebrity designers. But just knowing they were up there somewhere in the buildings that lined the avenue was enough for her. She didn't mind almost being mowed down by deliverymen hurriedly pushing metal hand trucks piled high with boxes destined for the offices of those very designers. It was all just part of the action.

Charlie and Emma turned right on 37th Street toward Laceland, carefully navigating around the black garbage bags and tied stacks of flattened cardboard boxes lining the curb.

Emma frowned. "You're not helping! I have to figure out a way to call Paige

Young back. She left two messages last night, and it's already three-thirty. I don't want Allegra to seem rude."

Charlie threw all of his weight into pulling open the massive front door of the office building as Emma walked through.

"Hey, Allegra Biscotti is a very busy woman. Personally, I think it's a good thing that she didn't call Paige back right away. You don't want her to seem desperate or anything, do you?"

"I guess not." Emma stopped talking as other people stepped into the elevator with them. Once they were safely on the Laceland floor, she continued. "But I think Allegra needs to respond today."

"Agreed. Paige left her cell-phone number, right?"

Emma nodded. "Yeah."

"So, why doesn't she—you, whoever—just send Paige a text?" Charlie suggested.

Emma pursed her lips and thought for a second. "Is that, like, professional?"

"What are you two plotting now?" Marjorie asked from behind the file cabinet as Emma and Charlie entered the reception area of Laceland.

Emma felt a twinge of nervousness in her stomach. She hadn't seen Marjorie there. Had she heard what they were talking about? She wasn't sure how her dad would feel about her pretending to be an Italian fashion designer to his client. Her guess—not thrilled.

Marjorie slid the file drawer shut with her hip and stepped back around to her desk. "Figuring out how to stuff the ballot box to get Charlie elected to student council, perhaps?"

Emma let out her breath, relieved. Marjorie clearly had no idea what they were talking about. "Something like that," Emma answered as Charlie stifled a snort.

"Can you continue your strategy session while you cover the phones? It's time for my caffeine fix. I'm *dying*."

Without waiting for Emma's response, Marjorie pulled her purse out of the bottom drawer and reached for her nubby, turquoise tweed swing coat on the coatrack.

"Have fun, kids. Don't do anything I wouldn't do!"

Charlie settled himself in the vinyl guest chair to the side of the reception desk. "As I was about to say, a text message is professional. Everybody does it now. Even old people."

"My grandma doesn't," Emma countered.

Charlie shot her a look. "I didn't mean *that* old. But like adults and stuff."

"Okay, fine. So what should we *write* in the text? Am I letting her buy the dress? How would that whole thing work? Does Allegra take checks or what? I have a bank account, but I can't deposit a check made out to Allegra, can I?"

Charlie leaned back and propped his feet up on Marjorie's desk. "Good point. That could get complicated."

"Could we...I dunno...could we give it to her? I know her size, and I'm almost finished with it anyway," Emma suggested. "Or is that just weird, like she'll think Allegra is trying to bribe her or something?"

"No! I mean, yes! I mean no, it's not weird, and yes, you could give it to her. I think designers give things to fashion editors and celebrities all the time. It's called 'gifting.' My mom is friends with some actresses who have been on TV and in movies, and I've heard them talking about how they get tons of stuff for free. Sometimes designers just send things, and sometimes celebrities go to these gift lounges and they can pick anything they want. Designers want stars to be photographed in their clothes."

"Stars maybe, but fashion editors? Really?" Emma asked.

"Yeah...I mean, I think so." Charlie leaned forward and stared for a second at some far-off spot. Emma could see his scheming mind at work, churning through all the angles, all the possibilities.

"If you give something to an editor it's not like she *has* to write about it in the magazine," Charlie continued. "Besides, Paige has already plugged your clothes. So you could just think of giving her the dress like a thank-you-slash-engagement present. Why do you think fashion editors are dressed so well all the time? It's called perks."

The office phone rang, and Emma put up her finger to silence Charlie. She put on her best Marjorie voice. "Good afternoon! Laceland Distributors. Emma speaking. May I help you?" Emma crossed her eyes at Charlie while she listened to the voice on the other end of the line.

"I believe that Isaac is out on a delivery. May I take a message?"

Emma carefully wrote down the information on the old-school pink "While You Were Out" notepad that Marjorie insisted on using. Laceland was still very low-tech in many ways.

"See?" Charlie said, pointing both of his index fingers at her. "You do an almost perfect Marjorie imitation. Your voice isn't as gravelly as hers, but it's close. If you really wanted to, you could fake Allegra's voice."

Emma couldn't help but laugh. "No impersonations. I'm trying to be a designer, not a stand-up comedian," she said.

She loved that Charlie was so unlike the other boys in school. He was quirky and funny and just comfortable to be with—more like a brother who was the same age than a boy-boy. Ever since Emma had met Charlie in the fourth grade, she'd never felt weird or nervous around him the way she did with guys like Jackson. He had always been just Charlie, and they were just friends, and their friendship was just something that never had to be analyzed or discussed or made into something more. It was easy…even if Charlie himself wasn't always so easy.

"All right, so we'll gift the dress to Paige," she agreed. "But how should we get it to her so she doesn't know it's coming from Emma instead of Allegra?"

"We can deliver it ourselves," he suggested. "There's probably a messenger center at the magazine. We'll just drop it off. She won't even know who brought it."

Emma thought over the whole thing for a minute. It *sounded* like it could work. But then again, Charlie could make even the most impossible thing sound like it could work. The only other option was not to do it. And that meant going back to just being Emma, sewing dresses in a corner of her father's lace warehouse.

"All right, let's do it." She glanced over at the wall clock and pulled her cell phone out of her bag. "Roll your chair over here. Let's write this text message before it gets too late."

After ten minutes and many more false starts, Emma and Charlie were finally satisfied with their message:

Ms. Young, Thx 4 ur msgs. I did c the blog postings & am v. appreciative. As 4 the dress, pls look 4 a special delivery 2 ur office 2morrow. Best, AB

"Perfect!" Charlie said.

Emma's finger hovered over the green button on her phone, but she just couldn't pull the trigger. Suddenly her palms were sweaty. She put down the phone to rub her hands on her jeans.

"Em? Are you gonna send it or what?" Charlie asked.

"It's just...well, this is a big deal. It's the first thing Allegra has ever said, her very first conversation!"

Charlie smiled. "Kind of like a baby's first word?"

"I know I'm being lame, but suddenly Allegra is becoming a real person. She designs clothes and gets messages from an important fashion editor and has pictures of her dresses on the Web...plus, I'm a little freaked out," she admitted.

"Paige Young is going to be so stoked that she's gonna be the first person ever to wear an original Allegra Biscotti design. She won't think twice about the stupid text message. Seriously. Okay?"

"Okay." Emma pressed send.

Charlie stood. "The second Marjorie gets back and unchains you from the desk, you should finish the dress."

The dress. *Charlie's right*, Emma realized. *It's all about the dress.*

In her cozy studio, surrounded by her tins full of buttons and ribbons and a rainbow of scraps from the beautiful things she'd made with her very own hands, the anxiety building up inside her disappeared. Now she was just excited.

She could already picture Paige wearing the raspberry halter dress—*her* dress. Maybe Paige would tie the sash on

the side, or right in the center—or knot it in the back to make it her very own. Maybe she'd even get photographed in it at some fancy fashion-industry party. How cool would that be?

Or maybe she would come out of the bathroom wearing it on the first day of her honeymoon, and her new husband would be blown away at the sight of her. Maybe he would say that she had never looked prettier. And maybe—just maybe—Paige would remember that moment for the rest of her life.

SPECIAL DELIVERY

Emma hugged the carefully wrapped package that held the Allegra Biscotti dress—the first one that was going to be worn by an actual person instead of just a dress form—against her chest. She tipped her head back, looking skyward at the impossibly tall and sleek-angled all-glass building that housed *Madison* magazine.

"You coming?" Charlie asked, as he pushed one of the three massive, revolving glass doors leading into the building. Emma hurried to catch up.

The spacious marble lobby crackled with energy and activity. Several women and a few men stood speaking into their cell phones. The women quickly strolling in and out of glass revolving doors wore narrow pencil skirts in an array of neutrals—grays, blacks, browns, and beiges—no bright colors, as far as Emma could tell, and super high-heeled strappy shoes in rich-looking suede, exotic speckled skins, and here and there a metallic shimmer.

Cashmere wraps and fabulously cut jackets were thrown

over shoulders just so—it was as if each and every woman walking through the lobby was camera-ready. Even the men were photo-shoot ready. Their navy-blue and slate-gray suits were slim and fitted, with a dash of color in the ties—subtly textured pastel lilac and eye-popping fuchsia.

Visitors lined up at the front desk between two red velvet ropes, as if trying to get into an exclusive party instead of attend a meeting in the offices upstairs. Messengers—some in neon spandex bike gear—crowded around the far end of the security desk in a less organized way, jostling each other so they could drop off their packages and make the rest of their deliveries before businesses closed for the day.

A shiver ran up Emma's spine. This is the real deal, she thought. This lobby *oozed* fashion.

Emma looked down at her nautical navy-and-white boat-neck top and jeans and then over at Charlie's chunky black sweater and red classic Chucks.

"We don't exactly fit in."

"Who cares? We don't need to," Charlie replied, filled with confidence as usual. Still, Emma wished she had thought to go home and change into something more stylish.

She stared across the lobby at a tall woman in an African-print minidress with a huge collar. Even from this distance, Emma could see the dress was runway-worthy. Amazing, really. The package in her arms suddenly felt strangely heavy, as if she were a child lugging home her beloved preschool art project.

"This place is sort of giving me the creeps."

"I think we have to go over there with the other messengers." Charlie headed toward the security desk.

"Okay." Emma wished she could pull out her sketchbook. The Game would be really easy to play here. She turned to follow Charlie.

"You can *not* be serious!"

Emma froze. Paige Young stood five feet in front of her.

"*I* am *not* taking a *subway* down to Tribeca with all these garment bags," Paige told a twenty-something girl with a super-high ponytail and the skinniest pants Emma had ever seen. Paige covered the phone speaker with her hand and focused on the girl.

"I thought you confirmed the car service. 'Confirmed' means calling an hour before the pickup time to make sure they have the booking, not just checking to see that you have it down on my calendar."

Ponytail Girl quaked in her stacked-heel boots. "I-I can call them now..." the girl who must be Paige's assistant stammered.

"*He-llo!* It's Friday afternoon! The chances of them being

able to send a car in the next ten..." Paige looked down at her gold watch, "make that *five* minutes are slim to none, and none just left town in a stretch limo."

Paige put the phone back up to her ear. "I'm so, so sorry, Pierre!" she said, her tone instantly shifting from an irritated growl to a sweet coo. "*S'il vous plaît excusez-moi.* I will be at the photo shoot as soon as humanly possible. Yes, yes—breaking in a new assistant. Ah, so you understand. Ciao, Pierre!"

Emma was fascinated. She couldn't stop from openly staring, as if watching some sort of improv theater performance. Pass the popcorn—she was set.

Charlie came up beside her. "What happened? I thought you were right behind me. I was almost at the front of the—"

"Shhh!" Emma nodded her head toward Paige, who had ended her call.

"That's her!" Charlie exclaimed, before Emma could gag him.

Paige's gaze shifted quickly over to Charlie and then back to Emma. "Hey! Aren't you—?"

Emma's first instinct was to run. Fast. They had learned about animals' flight-or-fight responses in biology. And she was most definitely a fleer. But Charlie blocked her path to the door.

He moved in front of Emma and smiled. "Allegra Biscotti's interns. We met at Laceland earlier in the week." He sounded smooth and confident.

God, what acting skills, Emma thought. Either his mother

had taught him well, or it was in his genes. Emma didn't care which as long as Charlie stayed in control, because she sure had no idea what to say.

"Actually, Ms. Young, we're here to deliver a package to you from Allegra Biscotti," he continued.

Emma slightly raised the package—for protection as much as proof.

Paige pursed her mauve lips and blinked a couple of times. "I'm kind of on my way out—if I can manage to find a taxi or horse-drawn carriage or one of those stupid bicycle cabs to get me downtown before the photographer walks off the set," she said, narrowing her eyes at her ponytailed assistant, who rapidly typed on her phone in a flurry of concentrated activity.

"Caroline." Ponytail Girl jolted into ready position. "Take this package up to my office when you return."

Emma stared for a moment at the girl's outstretched hand. She wanted Paige to have the dress. She did. But not like this.

She had been expecting something different. A gasp, knowing she had gotten the beloved dress. Oprah-like exclamations of joy. Happiness.

She shifted the package in her arms. Her clothes were joyful things. They made her happy. She knew that sounded odd, but Paige just wasn't in the right mind-set now. Emma couldn't loosen her grasp.

"Thank you," Paige prompted, shooting Emma a quizzical look.

Charlie nudged her hard with his elbow.

Emma slowly released the package. She watched as Ponytail Girl casually tucked it under her arm and then held the screen of her phone toward Paige.

"We got it! A car is coming down the street now."

Paige headed for the front doors without a glance back at Emma or Charlie.

Emma hoped she had done the right thing. Would this woman like her dress? Love it? Wear it? Even care?

Emma slowly followed Charlie back onto the street, letting herself get swept up in the growing crowd of tourists taking over Times Square.

"Okay. Pause. What was that about?" Charlie demanded.

Emma couldn't even begin to find the words to explain how it felt to part with her dress.

"Whatever. It's your deal, but I think it went well," he said, clearly satisfied with their mission.

"You don't think us being there made Paige suspicious or anything, do you?"

Charlie waved his hand as they stopped at a crosswalk. "Nah. Our story was totally believable. Besides, it seemed like Paige had more important stuff to worry about. She's totally forgotten about us by now."

"Hopefully," Emma said. "You know, if she doesn't go back to the office tonight, she might not get the dress until Monday morning."

"So?"

"It's a long time to wait." Emma tore at a hangnail on her thumb. "I'm just saying, that's all."

"Just think how happy she'll be when she gets into the office after the weekend and finds the dress inside," Charlie replied, always the optimist.

"I just hope she likes it as much as she thought she did." Emma now feared that her dress wouldn't live up to Paige's first sighting. Under the harsh fluorescent lights of the magazine's office, the dress might look...ordinary.

They crossed Broadway. Street vendors set up along the sidewalk sold knockoffs of designer handbags, books, jewelry, and souvenirs from folding tables. Charlie stopped.

"Look at these awesome old concert T-shirts." He rifled through a stack of shirts. "Beastie Boys, Tears for Fears, Frankie Goes to Hollywood, the English Beat, the Go-Go's?

I've never heard of any of these bands. Oh wait, I think I know the Cure."

"Who cares?" Emma said, feeling her mood turning. Clothing did that to her. "The graphics on them are so blocky and retro. I could totally do something fun with these." She glanced at the crudely lettered sign: *12 for $25*. "Help me pick."

A half an hour later, Emma sat cross-legged on her bedroom floor, while Charlie played a video game on her computer and munched on stale pretzels he'd pilfered from the kitchen. Sorting the shirts by color—black-gray, red, white, yellow-orange-pink, green-blue-purple—was working to calm her down.

"So what's your master plan?" Charlie asked, nudging the stack of shirts with his foot.

Emma reached for her fabric shears. "I was thinking about cutting out the band logos and sewing them onto plain T-shirts. You staying?"

"Definitely." He turned back to the computer. "Mom's holding an acting workshop at our place tonight. Ten women sitting around practicing how to cry realistically on cue for three hours."

"Sounds brutal." Emma began cutting. She didn't want all

her patches to be squares or rectangles. She trimmed around the outline of the artwork on each shirt instead.

"It's one of her most popular classes," Charlie explained. "She gets to charge extra. That's good." Charlie didn't have to say more. Emma knew his mom hadn't landed many parts lately, even though she was always going out on auditions. His mom had once been a big deal—part of the original Broadway cast of *Rent*—but she couldn't get cast these days. Charlie didn't like to talk about it.

Emma retrieved a gray T-shirt from the bin on top of the dryer and placed a Rolling Stones big lips logo on top of it, then played around with pieces of other logos to see what worked together.

"So what's Holls up to this weekend?" Charlie asked.

"Get this. Apparently she's going to a teen yoga class with Ivana tomorrow." Emma waited for the humor to sink in.

Charlie snorted. "You're lying!"

"Am not. Swear to Chanel. I couldn't believe it when she told me either. She *never* exercises except by force in gym class."

Emma tilted her head and considered the arrangement of patches. That works, she decided. She reached for her sewing kit, took out some black embroidery thread, and started threading a needle. "But the weird thing was that when I made a teeny, tiny joke about it, she got all defensive. She said I was making fun of her. What's that about? How could she not see that her suddenly going to a yoga class is at least *kind of* funny? She never used to be that hyper-sensitive."

"I know what you mean," Charlie agreed. "I think I've seen and spoken to her even less than you have—and I don't have an after-school job. And when I do see her, it's like she forgot how to talk."

Emma finished sewing on the first patch. She held it up to see how it looked. It's pretty good, she thought, but I should make the sewing rawer, not so neat and even. She re-threaded the needle and picked up another patch.

"I should probably try harder to like Ivana for Holly's sake, but I just…can't. The thing is that I don't want to not be friends with Holly either. I miss her. But these days, I kind of miss her even when she's sitting right next to me."

Charlie shook his head slowly. "You girls are so complicated."

"Tell me about it."

Her dad popped his head in the door. "Cookie, I'm home. I'm going to start dinner soon. Can you set the table?"

"Isn't it Will's turn?" Emma asked. "I'm kind of in the middle of something."

"Nope. He did it last night." Her dad walked into the room and picked up a black INXS T-shirt. "Wow, this sure brings me back."

"It does? To what?" Emma asked. "You know these bands?"

"Anyone home?" her mother called from the hallway.

"In Emma's room!" her dad answered.

"Hi, everyone." Her mom slumped in the doorway, rumpled and tired from her day. Emma took one look at her mom and decided to make her a new tote with her gel pens…anything to liven up that drab wardrobe!

"Taking a break from studying for the Western civ exam?" her mom asked Emma.

Emma gritted her teeth. Her mom never let up.

"It's *Friday*, Mom."

Her dad grabbed an R.E.M. shirt off the floor.

"Joanie, look at this! Remember this concert?"

Her mom took the shirt out of his hands. A smile transformed her face.

"Yes! Wow, I haven't thought about that night in years."

"What happened?" Emma asked.

"Oh, nothing," her dad said slyly. "Just that your mother sweet-talked our way into a sold-out R.E.M. concert. She faked a Southern accent and pretended she was the lead singer's slightly demented sister."

"Noah!" Joan batted his arm playfully and blushed.

"No way!" Emma exclaimed. She couldn't match up the clog-wearing, schoolteacher mom in front of her with a girl sneaking into a concert with her boyfriend.

"And then she got us invited to the after-party," Emma's father added with a wide grin. "By the end of the night, I think Michael Stipe thought you really were his sister!"

Her mother laughed. "I forgot about that part. He was adorable, that's for sure. I don't think I ever got over that crush, even after he shaved his hair off. That was a wild night."

"One of the best," her dad agreed.

Emma knitted her eyebrows together and watched these new alien parents beam at each other, reliving their happy moment. She couldn't believe her mom had partied with the band all night. Emma could kind of see her dad doing that. He was way more relaxed than her mom. He liked to joke around and play harmless practical jokes on people.

But her mom was so serious all the time—so all about academics. What other wild things had her mom done? And why had she stopped doing them?

"You can have the shirt if you want," Emma offered.

Her mom smiled. "No, thanks. You keep it. It's not really my style, and it doesn't look like it would fit me anyway. I'm going to go change and help your dad with dinner."

Her parents shared a private laugh as they left the room.

Emma loved that a random piece of clothing could transport her parents to another place and time. A very different place and time...

THE WOMAN BEHIND THE DRESS

Monday was almost over, and Emma still hadn't heard a peep out of Paige.

She must've gotten the dress by now, Emma thought as she walked to her locker after her last class. *Or maybe not. Maybe she spent the day out of the office at another photo shoot or visiting a designer's showroom. Maybe she's at home with the flu. Or maybe she hates it. Maybe the other editors are gathered around her right now, mocking her for featuring the dress on her blog.*

Emma tried to delete that recurring thought.

There could be a million good reasons why Paige hasn't called yet, Emma decided. She opened her locker, grabbed her messenger bag, and pulled out her phone.

There was a text message. From Paige.

Pleasebegood, pleasebegood, pleasebegood, Emma wished. She flipped open the phone.

> Thx so much 4 the dress! I ADORE it. I'd love 2 speak with u ASAP. I wld like 2 interview u 4 Madison magazine. Pls let me know when is convenient. Paige Young

Emma tried to steady herself as kids streamed around her in the hallway, completely unaware of how the earth was shifting under her feet at this very moment. Paige liked the dress. No, she *adored* it. That meant that she would wear it. And now *Madison* magazine wants to interview *me?* I mean, Allegra?

Emma caught sight of Charlie's white-blond hair down the hallway.

"Charlie!" Emma shouted. "*Char-lie!*"

But no matter how loudly she called his name over the sounds of slamming lockers and chattering students who were finally free for the day, he didn't turn around. She was too far away for him to hear her. She jogged down the hallway, bobbing and weaving, running an obstacle course to get to him as six strands of vintage art-glass beads banged against her chest.

"Whoa! What the...? Em, what's up? You practically knocked me over," Charlie said.

"You've. Got. To. See. This. " Emma directed him over to the wall of the front foyer and shoved her phone in his hand.

"Are you kidding me with this?" Charlie exclaimed. "This is awesome!"

"Yeah," Emma said, beaming. "Except..."

"Except what?"

"I don't know." Emma wrinkled her nose. "I guess I never thought about what would happen after. I mean, I just thought

Paige would get the dress, hopefully be happy, say thank you, and that'd be it. But an interview? I don't know about that."

"Are you crazy? An interview is good."

Emma wasn't sure it was good. "But I'm not an Italian fashion designer. I'm me. In middle school. I don't know what I'm doing. Maybe I should just fess up, you know, before this goes any further."

"Whaaat? No. No way, Em. Not now. Her asking to interview Allegra is a *good* thing. Telling her that Allegra doesn't exist and that we were tricking her would be a *bad* thing."

"I don't know. I feel weird pretending Allegra is a real person." Emma's lunch started doing ballroom-dancing moves in her stomach. She leaned against the wall.

"Allegra *is* a real person! She's *you*. You designed those dresses. So we're not really tricking Paige at all. Isn't this what you want? To be a fashion designer—a real one?"

"Well, yes—"

"So then you can't stop now." Charlie's eyes glinted. "You handle the fashion stuff. Let me do the other stuff. Come on. It'll be fun. We'll be partners in crime. I mean, really, nothing good is happening around here." He gestured to the empty hallways.

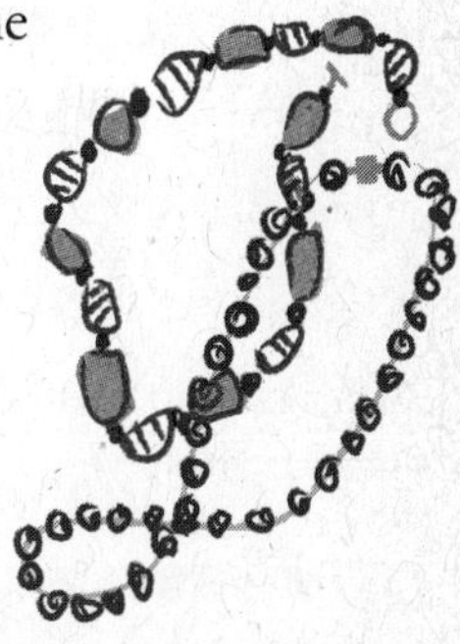

Emma closed her eyes and imagined the raspberry dress on Paige. Maybe

Charlie's right, she thought. After all, I did design those dresses, she reasoned. Allegra is me.

Emma snapped opened her eyes at the sound of typing—on her phone. Before she could speak or dive for the phone, Charlie pressed send.

Emma gasped. "What did you just do?" She snatched the phone away and read the sent text:

> Ms. Young, I'm v. busy working on my new collection. Pls text ur questions & I will respond accordingly. All best, AB

"See?" Charlie said. "Problem solved."

Emma widened her eyes at Charlie. "I can't believe you just did that!"

"Can't believe how obnoxious I was for sending a message to Paige without asking you first, or can't believe how genius my response was?" Charlie grinned.

"Both."

Charlie linked arms with Emma as they stepped outside. "What are you doing for the rest of the day?" he asked.

Just then, Emma's phone vibrated in her hand. She and Charlie stopped. And then it vibrated again. And again. Three new text messages…four…five.

Emma gazed at the screen. All questions for Allegra Biscotti.

"Um, apparently, being interviewed by the editor of New York's hottest glossy!" Emma beamed.

"And we're off!" Charlie announced happily. "Here. Sit. We'll bang out these answers in no time. This is wild!" He jabbed her arm playfully.

"Beyond." Emma couldn't help but feel her cheeks burn with excitement.

They hung their bags on the peeling railing, sat on the concrete steps of the school, and huddled over Emma's phone.

Charlie scrolled back to the first text. "Okay, first question: 'Where were you born and/or where did you grow up?' Allegra's Italian, right?"

"I don't know about that," Emma replied. "I mean, maybe she's American or even a New Yorker. Paige *did* discover Allegra's dresses in the Garment District after all. If she was Italian, wouldn't she be living and designing in Italy? Besides, we have to make her story believable, don't you think?"

"Believable is boring," Charlie countered.

"True," Emma agreed. "And Allegra is *not* boring! Her designs are 'fresh' and 'playful' and 'imaginative,' just like Paige wrote in her blog."

"Not that you memorized her review or anything," Charlie teased.

"I think Allegra deserves a supercool, creative story." Emma closed her eyes and tried to picture the Woman Behind the Clothes. It was the first time she'd let herself

do that since coming up with the name Allegra Biscotti.

"I know what we should write!" Charlie exclaimed. He grabbed Emma's phone. He must've seen the horror on Emma's face, because he added, "Don't worry! I'll show it to you for approval before I send!"

"Go ahead," she said. She wouldn't admit it out loud, but he was good at this stuff.

When Charlie finished typing, he handed the phone to Emma.

She read his message out loud: "I'm a citizen of the world. I'm the daughter of a U.S. diplomat. We lived in Europe, Asia, South America—you name it. I've dined with royalty and slept in the desert."

Emma giggled. She loved that her alter ego was so worldly. The only place Emma had been out of the country was Canada, and that didn't really count.

"I love it. Approved!" she said. A thrill went through her as she pressed send.

Charlie took back the phone and read the next question: "'Who are your design influences?'" He typed and then showed the screen to Emma. "All of the biggies," he had written.

"What? No!" Emma grabbed the phone from him. Clearly his one-answer streak was already over. "Allegra would never say 'biggies'!" Emma deleted Charlie's response and started again.

> I live in NYC & I luv the boldness & freshness of American culture—the colors, the food, and mostly the people!

"All right, I'll give that one to you," Charlie said, "but I think Allegra has to name some designers to sound legit."

Emma tapped the phone against her chin. Charlie was actually right. But how was she going to narrow down her list of favorite designers to just 160 characters or less? But really the answer was simple. When she thought about the person she most aspired to be like, only one name popped into her mind.

> Coco Chanel: the ultimate classic.

"What's next?" she asked, giving Charlie the phone.

"Okay, let's see. 'How would you describe your design sensibilities?'"

Emma frowned. "Can we come back to that one?"

"No! Come on, Em. You're on a roll! This should be the easiest one for you."

But Emma just shook her head.

"Fine. Be that way." Charlie jumped back into the driver's seat. "How about this?" he asked, showing her what he had just typed.

> The fantastical fashion fantasies of a young woman who can't wait 4 her big moment in the spotlight when she's all dressed up w/EVERYWHERE 2 go!

Emma paused. Her skin was tingling, like a thousand tiny stars were dancing all over her body. "Charlie! That's amazing and so...so true! But won't Paige know it's me? I mean, me, Emma?"

"Negatory," he said, pressing send with confidence. "Next: 'At what age did you start designing?'"

"Awesome! We don't even have to make up an answer to that one." Emma took the phone from his hand and started tapping away.

> I spoke the language of fashion even b4 I knew how 2 talk. I've been adding a new word to my style vocabulary every day since. I hope 2 never stop.

The doors behind them suddenly burst open. A bunch of soccer players sporting their team uniforms appeared, juggling duffel bags and soccer balls.

Jackson Creedon was one of them.

As he passed, Emma couldn't help but notice how strong Jackson's legs looked in his soccer shorts—which were unfortunately made out of an awful shiny red-and-white polyester—and his black-and-white striped soccer cleats. He paused at the bottom of the steps to tie his shoe. Emma blushed and looked down at her hands, so he wouldn't catch her staring at him again.

"Heads up!" someone called out.

Before Emma knew what was happening, a stray soccer ball landed in her lap—right on top of her open, sweaty palms. Even though she could feel the team's eyes on her, she stared at the ball, frozen in place and blushing madly. Is Jackson looking at me, too? Emma wondered.

Part of her was desperate to look up and find out, but the other part was terrified of meeting his eyes in front of all of his sporty friends...in front of Charlie. How is it that I can suddenly be so freaked out—or is it excited?—when Jackson is within ten feet of me, Emma wondered, but I don't feel a thing when Charlie is practically sitting on top of me or hanging out in my bedroom?

A boy who Emma hadn't even noticed was suddenly standing right next to her. He gingerly tapped the ball out of her lap with his toe, sending it flying. Jackson and his teammates raced for the ball, starting an impromptu volley as they scampered down the sidewalk, passing the ball back and forth between them, and dodging around pedestrians. The boys were probably headed toward the school fields on the next block. It must be a game day.

"What's up with him?" Charlie asked, nodding in Jackson's general direction.

"Nothing," Emma croaked. She coughed and spoke again in hope of making her answer sound more convincing. "Nothing."

"Really? Then why were you acting as if someone Tasered you the minute he came outside?" Charlie asked.

"No big reason." Emma shrugged. "I just didn't expect the ball to wind up in my lap, that's all. What if it had hit me in the head? I could've gotten a concussion or something."

"Doubtful, but whatever," Charlie said, reaching for his bag. "Hey, when you get home, you should write all this stuff down in case Allegra gets asked to do another interview."

Emma laughed as she took her bag from him. "Come on, get real. Paige is so not going to buy this stuff. She has met zillions of fashion designers. She's never going to believe 'I am a citizen of ze world!'"

"Does Allegra have an accent now? We didn't discuss that part. We should probably work on getting our stories straight," Charlie joked as he started down the steps.

"Charlie, I'm being serious!"

"Well, why shouldn't Paige believe it? I think Allegra's answers were really good. And Em, for the most part, they were all *true*. Paige loves Allegra's clothes, or she wouldn't keep trying to find out more about her. Right? Besides, what's the worst that can happen?"

STYLE SHOWDOWN

These gold leggings are amazing!" Kayla gushed. "Look at the cute zipper at the ankle!"

"I don't know, Kay," Ivana said. "Not everyone can get away with leggings."

A glittery-pink frown quickly spread across Kayla's glossed lips. She let the leggings swing back into line with the rest of the clothes on the rack.

Only twenty minutes in, and Emma had long since moved past the shock that she was actually spending a Saturday shopping at Bloomingdale's with Ivana and the Ivana-Bees. Annoyance had come and gone, too. At this point, the best she figured she could hope for was numbness. The frustrating thing was that she had no one to blame but herself.

When Holly first suggested a group shopping quest a couple of days earlier, Emma could tell she fully expected Emma to say no. But it seemed like the perfect chance to make good on her private promise to try harder with Holly's friends. Maybe, she hoped, Ivana was one of those girls who acted totally differently outside school. And Emma had to admit she'd loved the look of genuine happiness on Holly's face when she said she'd go.

Besides, Emma liked Bloomie's, with its bright lights and art-deco, black-and-white-checkered shiny tiled floor. Following the girls through the maze of the cosmetics department to reach the escalator, she'd inhaled the overwhelming scent of perfume, which had brought her back to the yearly fall pilgrimage with Mom to buy an itchy dress coat for the holidays.

"Let's go to the boutiques on the top floor," Emma had suggested, as they entered and ascended the escalator in a pack.

"Can *you* afford Gucci?" Ivana literally looked down on her from her spot two steps above.

Emma could feel her face turning red. "I just like to look."

"Yeah, well, *we* like to shop," Ivana said. "It's way more fun."

Emma glanced over at Holly, hoping she'd back her up. Or at least share an eye-roll. But Holly was staring intently over the edge of the escalator, down at a rack of multi-striped scarves as if there were going to be a pop quiz on their stripe patterns at the top.

So Emma and the girls got off at the trendy floor.

One identically cut piece after another, Emma thought, as she flipped through seemingly endless racks of straight-leg stretchy jeans and solid-color sweaters without a single interesting design detail.

"Oooh, how about these?" Shannon asked the group, holding up a pair of leggings that were fashioned to look like jeans. Emma held back a shudder. Horrible, they were just horrible.

Ivana stepped over to inspect. "These are pretty good," she declared. "They're not *my* kind of thing exactly, but they could work on you. Maybe they'd make you look like you have some curves."

Lexie pulled out a long, clingy T-shirt with a low-cut V-neck in a silver and black stretch material.

"What about this?" she asked, holding it up to her body. She cocked her head to look at herself in a mirror. "Hot or not?"

"Totally hot!" Shannon said.

"Yes!" Kayla agreed, nodding like a bobble-head doll. "Your body would look killer in that top. And I could do your makeup! My mom just gave me this new eyeliner that's all sparkly. It would look great with your dark brown eyes."

"You could wear that cute fedora you just got with it," Holly added. "You know, to add a little mystery."

It took all of Emma's strength not to let a look of disgust

overwhelm her face. Why was Holly fawning all over Lexie like that?

Lexie continued admiring herself, clearly not ready to give up the spotlight just yet.

"Do you think Jackson would like it?"

"Jackson is going to flip." Shannon giggled.

"He might like it," Ivana added. "Or, he might not."

Emma stiffened. Maybe she was imagining it, but Emma swore that Ivana had just given her a knowing look. What if Holly had spilled the beans and told Ivana that Emma was interested in Jackson? No, Holly wouldn't do that, Emma reasoned. She would *never* betray Emma's trust like that... would she?

"I don't know," Lexie said, returning the top to the rack. "I think I can do better."

"Than Jackson or the shirt?" Ivana quipped, sending the 'Bees into giggles.

As the girls moved on, Emma trailed behind. She was bored with the racks and racks of jeans, leggings, draped cotton tops, and long V-necked cardigans that she was sure were already in healthy supply in each of the girls' closets. There has to be a way to make this more fun, she thought.

"Hey, you guys," Emma began hesitantly. "How about we be each others' fashion stylists? We could put together outfits for each other and then put on a little fashion show in the dressing room."

"I love that idea!" Holly enthused. She gave Emma a supportive look.

"So fun!" Shannon said.

"I think so, too," Kayla added.

There was no mistaking Ivana's look of annoyance as the girls grew excited about Emma's idea. Clearly *she* didn't think this was the greatest idea ever.

"That could *definitely* be fun, but I think we could make it even more interesting," she said, the power and volume of her voice commanding everyone's attention back to her. "Why don't we turn it into a little friendly competition? I don't know...like maybe me against Emma, and the best stylist wins."

Emma swallowed hard. She couldn't believe that Ivana was challenging her. But if I can win at anything, I can win at a style showdown.

"Let's do it," she replied.

"Great," Ivana said. "Now we need to choose models. Since it was my idea, I pick first. Okay?"

"Sure," Emma said.

The girls—including Holly, Emma noticed with shock—posed and preened to show Ivana their modeling skills.

"Umm, I want...Lexie," Ivana declared. Lexie yipped with pleasure and bounded over to Ivana's side.

"Holly," Emma said. Holly would've automatically been Emma's first choice no matter what, but Emma couldn't shake off the vibe that Holly seemed disappointed that Ivana hadn't picked her.

"What about me and Shaye?" Kayla asked Ivana.

"You two are the judges," Ivana instructed. "Okay, then. How about Emma and I get twenty minutes to pick clothes for our models?"

"I only need fifteen," Emma countered confidently. If anyone has the advantage here, it's me, she thought. For once, she felt totally in control with Ivana.

"Fine. *Fifteen* minutes to grab clothes, then we meet back in the dressing room—the one by the coat section because that one has a little seating area with mirrors. We'll then get another ten minutes to dress our models. Does that work for everybody?" Ivana didn't bother waiting for answer. "Good. Let's go!"

"Holls, do you want to come with me?" Emma asked.

Holly glanced sideways at Lexie, Shannon, and Kayla. "Nah, I'll slow you down. We'll just wander around and meet you at the dressing room." She hesitated, as if she wanted to say more. "You good?"

Emma flashed a thumbs-up and took off.

She decided to go for a super-funky party look. She ran over to a rack displaying sparkly, sequined clothes. She quickly slid hangers across the rail until she found two totally cute skirts—a knee-length one that appeared to be made out of liquid gold and a mini covered in pink sequins.

These are completely great...but which one will look better on Holly? She held them up and gazed back and forth between them. *Both good*, she decided. She slung them over her arm. She'd figured it out later. The clock was ticking.

Okay, now I need something to counter the girliness of the skirts, Emma thought. *Something with a little edge*. She spun in a circle, scanning the mannequins set up on waist-high risers throughout the floor, hoping for a hint. Nothing jumped out at her.

Then she had an idea. She hopped on the escalator and jogged three flights up to the boys' department. She was looking for a sugar-and-spice, opposites-attract vibe.

A couple of steps into boyland, and she spotted exactly what she needed. T-shirts with cool, boldly colored Japanese anime characters like the ones in the comic books Charlie was obsessed with. Love these, she thought. Not what anyone would expect for a night out at all. She grabbed small sizes so they'd be very fitted on Holly.

She zoomed back to the escalator and checked the clock on her phone. Only five minutes left. Emma hurried down the moving steps, working her way around customers who preferred to lounge against the handrails while being carried to their destination.

Back on the second floor, Emma flew through the accessories department for a fistful of skinny, metallic, studded belts. She hung them over the crook of her elbow along with her other items. She darted into the shoe department, and knowing she wouldn't have time to wait for Holly's size, just grabbed two sample pairs of strappy sandals—in gold and silver—from the sale rack. Holly's toes could poke over the size-six sole.

Now I need a cute jacket for Holly to wear on top, Emma calculated as she headed back to the teen clothing area. Focusing her search on a long rack against the side wall, she nabbed a fierce black-denim jacket trimmed with tons of zippers; a cropped, swingy jacquard jacket with three-quarter-length sleeves; and a fuzzy, light-gray, mohair sleeveless cardigan sweater. One of these should do the trick, she thought.

At the last moment, she whisked a whisper-thin, long-sleeve

cream T-shirt and a flirty white ruffled tank off a nearby table—just in case. She burst through the entrance of the dressing room, somewhat out of breath.

Kayla and Shannon sat on a couch, flipping through the store catalog.

"You totally just made it," Kayla remarked. "You had like thirty seconds left."

Holly hurried over. "Wow! Look at all this stuff. Come on, I have a dressing room. Ivana and Lexie are already here styling."

Emma hung the different pieces around the dressing room as Holly stripped out of her winter white cords and roll-necked sweater and down to her underwear and bra.

"Do you think we'll win?" Holly asked.

"I could dress you in a shopping bag, and you'd look fabulous," Emma told her. It was true. Suddenly, Emma wished she had thought to let Holly try on the raspberry dress before she'd gifted it to Paige. Holly had the perfect body for it.

"I doubt it," Holly said, slipping into the gold skirt Emma had pulled off the hanger for her.

"Em, this totally reminds me of playing dress-up in my mom's closet. Remember?" Holly zipped herself in. The skirt fell perfectly, just as Emma knew it would.

Emma laughed. "*Of course,* I remember. A girl never forgets her first Chanel."

Holly's mom, who was a successful real-estate agent and a board member of many charities, had the most gorgeous clothes Emma had ever seen in one closet. A collection of black cocktail dresses in every imaginable fabric and style, elegant full-length gowns—a shimmery blue satin one that swept up and over one shoulder, a red chiffon one with cascading ruffles down the front and a short train in the back. For work, beautifully tailored suits lined in gemstone silk.

Best of all—and their favorite to try on—a classic Chanel skirt suit. It was made of pink-and-white-checked boucle wool with white fringed threads around all the edges and those fabulous signature double-C buttons.

The girls would lose themselves for hours in that closet. Then they'd strut over to Mrs. Richardson's vanity, where they'd top off their outfits with colorful jewels. Necklaces, bracelets, rings, and earrings. I bet some of those pieces were real, Emma now realized.

"That was so nice of your mom to let us play in her jewelry box," Emma reminded Holly, as she stepped into the pink sequined skirt.

They examined Holly's reflection in the three-way mirror. Both skirts looked totally great, but Emma knew she could only choose one.

"Which skirt do you like best?" Emma asked.

"This pink one," Holly said, tilting her head to the side. "It's so much cuter, and gold just isn't my thing—no offense."

Emma smiled at Holly in the mirror. "Then we'll go with pink."

Emma scanned the rest of her items to decide which pieces would work best with the pink skirt. First, she handed Holly the cream-colored, tissue-thin, long-sleeved shirt, and then she had her layer on a navy graphic T-shirt with a grinning character that looked like a cross between a rabbit, a mouse, and a small monkey. "The pink is going to look amazing with the navy."

"What's been going on with Jackson lately? Anything new?" Holly asked as she wriggled the tops over her head, one and then the other.

"Not really…well, sort of, I guess." Emma quickly told her about the soccer-ball incident, as she adjusted the layered shirts on Holly's body, scrunching up the sleeves of the long-sleeved tee.

"So did you guys talk?" Holly asked, her eyes glinting with anticipation.

"No…" Emma could see Holly frown slightly in the mirror, probably disappointed that there wasn't more to the story.

"But, um, I have these sketches. I mean, after I saw the team in those tacky polyester uniforms, I kind of reimagined them, made them sleeker."

Holly whirled around. "Do you have them with you? Let me see!"

Emma pulled her sketchbook out of her bag and flipped to the page.

Holly gasped and pointed to the face of the male figure wearing Emma's design. "Is that *Jackson?*"

Oh, no! Before Emma could grab the book away, Holly turned to the next page. It was covered with a half-dozen close-up sketches of Jackson's face. Emma suddenly felt like someone had just laid a steaming hot washcloth over her own face.

"These are really good, Em," Holly said sincerely. "These sketches look exactly like him. You're such a good artist. I'm so jealous. I can barely read my own handwriting, much less draw beautiful things."

"You think so?" Emma asked. "Well, actually, there's something else going on that's really cool—" Emma began.

But just at that moment, there was a loud knock on the dressing-room door. Emma grabbed back her sketchbook and shoved it deep in her bag.

"Come on, you guys!" Kayla called. "Fashion show is starting."

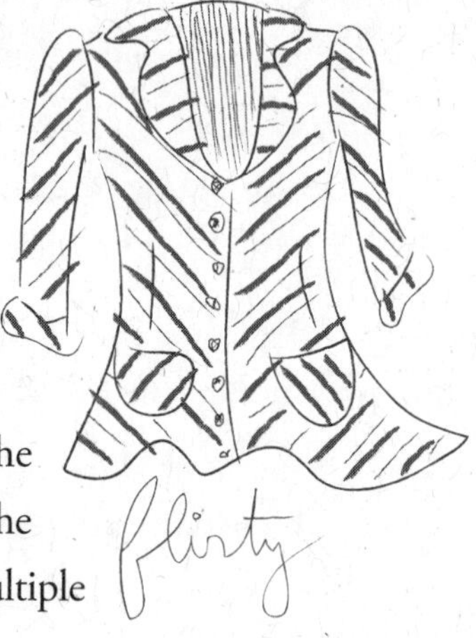

"Shoot! We're not done dressing you! Here, put this on," Emma instructed, handing Holly the gray mohair sweater. Then Emma grabbed three of the skinny belts—two she wrapped around Holly's waist, and the other she wound around her wrist multiple times as a makeshift cuff bracelet.

"Hmmm. Not perfect but good. Now all you have to do is make it down the 'runway' in these silver shoes. I'll see you out there. Good luck!"

Emma gave Holly a quick hug and then flung open the dressing-room door to join the other girls on the couch.

First up was Lexie, who shimmied down the hallway of the dressing room. She stopped in front of the girls and twirled, her long, dark hair fanning out in a circle, as she watched herself in the mirror. Emma could tell that Ivana had gone right to the high-priced designer section of the store and just picked the prettiest cocktail dress she saw—probably one that was already on a mannequin.

There was no denying that the strapless plum-colored satin dress looked gorgeous on Lexie. It had a flirty bustle in the back and a subtle sprinkling of crystals on the bodice, which pushed up Lexie's boobs. Definitely flattering, but it wasn't exactly imaginative. Lexie just looked like she was a well-dressed guest at some stuffy uptown hotel wedding.

Picking out a pretty dress and a rhinestone-encrusted evening purse wasn't exactly what Emma thought they were supposed to do. Where was the creativity in that?

Shannon and Kayla practically drooled over Ivana's outfit.

"Ivana, you have amazing taste!" Kayla gushed.

Shannon popped up from the couch to check out the price tag hanging from the back of Lexie's dress. "And *expensive* taste! I love it!"

Holly sashayed down the carpeted hall in her too-tight heels and then did the model-posing-at-the-end-of-the-catwalk thing—hand on right hip, hand on left hip—and then spun and walked back a few steps to end in a pretty pose. The pink sequins on her skirt glinted and sparkled. Emma knew that Holly was probably just goofing, but she definitely had what it took to be a real runway model.

Emma peeked at the judging panel. They stared blankly at Holly's outfit.

"I don't think those colors match," Kayla finally said with a frown.

"Colors don't always have to match as long as they go together," Emma explained. "See how the navy and pink work together? And the gray of the sweater plays off the silver studs on the belts and in the shoes?"

Kayla only shrugged.

"It seems weird to wear a big fuzzy sweater over a sequined skirt," Shannon said.

"I don't think so," Holly said. "Emma was just trying to mix different textures—right, Em? I think it's really fun."

Emma sank back into the couch. Holly could see what Emma was going for—or at least she was pretending to—so why didn't the other girls get it? Didn't they get that wearing clothes could be an art? How you could totally personalize clothes, even with things that weren't one of a kind, and could keep mixing things up endlessly to make them your own? That was the fun part!

"I know I'm not really supposed to talk or anything because I'm not one of the judges," Ivana said, so obviously about to break her own rule, "but Holls, let me just ask you. If you were invited to the hottest party of the year, would you pick Emma's outfit over the one I chose?"

"Um...I...uh," Holly stalled. "Well, it depends what kind of party it was, you know? This outfit might not be right for *all* occasions, but it could work for some things. Your outfit could kind of go anywhere."

Holly's eyes darted nervously to Emma's. Emma thought that Holly looked like a contestant on *American Idol* who had completely forgotten the lyrics. Emma actually felt bad for Holly, because Ivana had put her in a seriously lose-lose position. But she couldn't help but feel worse for herself since her best friend had just dissed her outfit to suck up to Ivana.

"You know, Emma really is a great designer with, like, totally natural talent," Holly said. "She can design anything. She just drew new soccer uniforms for the school team. Came up with the idea out of nowhere. You should see her sketches of Jackson wearing them. They're so hot!"

Emma's stomach dropped into her silver high-top sneakers. Did Holly really just say that?

"Hey, Lex! It looks like you got some competition over there," Ivana said, nodding in Emma's direction.

"Competition?" Lexie snorted. "You think?"

Kayla and Shannon giggled.

Emma had had enough. She raced back to the dressing room. All she wanted to do was get out of there.

"Em, wait!" Holly cried, bursting into the dressing room. "You didn't say your sketches were a secret. I just wanted everyone to see how awesome your stuff is. Don't make such a big deal about it, okay?"

"Sure…I get it," Emma said as evenly as she could,

avoiding Holly's eyes by putting the unused clothes back on their hangers. "No worries. I'm fine."

Emma suddenly felt frustrated—with Holly *and* herself. How can Holly hang out with these girls? They're not even nice to each other—and they're supposedly best friends—so why would I expect them to be nice to me? Emma wondered. She decided right there and then that she wasn't going to tell Holly about Allegra. What had just happened made it obvious that Holly was not keeping secrets from Ivana and the 'Bees these days.

The last thing I'm going to do, Emma silently vowed, is let Ivana ruin Allegra for me. Ivana can have her style-showdown victory and her lunch table and her loyal followers and even Holly's friendship—but she can't have this.

No way, Emma thought. Allegra is mine.

THREE NEW PIECES

Charlie calling her name from down the hallway just barely penetrated the fog Emma had been in for the thirty-six hours since the Bloomingdale's Incident. While Holly was acting as if nothing had happened, texting and chatting with Emma like usual, Emma couldn't shake the feeling that something—kind of big, actually—*had* happened. Every time she thought of Holly telling the group about her sketches of Jackson, Emma felt her stomach ballroom dance again. The fast stuff like sambas and tangos.

Now Emma stopped in her purple lace-up army boots—the ones she always wore when she needed a pick-me-up—so Charlie could catch up to her.

"Big news. And I mean, *huge*," he said.

"Like what? Like a new album by one of your freaky-weird European techno-bands was leaked online?"

Charlie considered that for a moment. "Well, yes, that'd be pretty awesome—but no. This is something you're actually going to *care* about."

He checked to the left and the right to make sure no one was listening and then leaned in close to Emma's ear. "Allegra's interview with Paige—*your* interview—was just published on the *Madison* website."

Emma's stomach upped the beat into cha-cha mode.

"Really? It was? How do you know?"

"Because I've been checking the website like twelve times a day. Haven't you?"

"Well, yeah, but not in the last hour. But, you're serious? You're not just saying this to cheer me up, are you?"

"Why would I do that? I'm not that insane. Go take a look. Now," he said.

"But how? I don't have study hall today."

"Simple. Just tell Mr. Singh you need a library pass. He'll give it to you. It's not like you'll miss much in his class. He takes so long to explain everything—"

Before Charlie could finish, Emma was already on her way down the hall. By some miracle, the library was practically empty. Emma grabbed the carrel facing away from Ms. Williams and brought up the *Madison* website. There on the home page was a teaser to the interview: "4 Fabulous Questions: A *Madison* Mini-Interview with Up-and-Coming Designer Allegra Biscotti."

She clicked open the page for the mini-interview. Along the side were the photos of her dresses that Paige took, and in the middle was the same headline as on the home page. Beneath the headline were the questions Paige had texted, each followed by Emma and Charlie's answers word for word, though taken out of text-speak and put into complete words and sentences.

Emma marveled at how Allegra Biscotti sounded smart, fashion-savvy, and worldly. When she had read over her responses last night, she worried that they sounded childish and silly. But even though what was on the site was practically the same as the original answers, they *seemed* different here. They made Allegra Biscotti *real.*

Emma floated back to class. Mr. Singh still seemed to be droning on about the same thing he had been when she'd left the room fifteen minutes earlier, giving Emma plenty of time to daydream: an Allegra Biscotti boutique in the West Village with a small, sunlit studio in the back to start...a show at New York Fashion Week...eventually a showroom on Fashion Avenue, her clothes in department stores across the country...

Then Paige Young storming Allegra's office, followed by a team of nervous editorial assistants and demanding to know the real identity of Allegra Biscotti...a photo of a disgraced Emma published on the front page of *Fashion News Daily*... her beautiful clothes being thrown out of apartment building windows by angry customers in protest...

Emma's mind spun around and around like a tornado forming in her head. Have Charlie and I gone too far? How much longer can we keep this going? What is Paige Young going to say—or worse, do—when she finds out that Allegra Biscotti doesn't exist, or really, that *I'm* Allegra Biscotti?

I should stop this, she decided.

Dear Paige, Emma began drafting in her head, I never meant to mislead you but—

The bell rang, snapping Emma out of her daze. Now, now, now—was all Emma could think—I have to take care of this now. She gathered her books in her arms and raced to her locker. She yanked her phone out of her bag, ready to type out the apology she had composed during class.

But it was too late.

A text from Paige was already waiting for her. Uh-oh. She beat me to it. Game over. Emma clicked open the text.

Ms. B: Requesting exclusive photo shoot of pieces from AB collection 2 b featured in upcoming print edition of Madison, Designers 2 Watch section. Interested?

Emma needed several seconds to process the fact that Paige

was not accusing her of pretending to be Allegra Biscotti. Instead, this was the exact opposite.

She wants what?...but I don't...I can't...now what?... how could I not...but I shouldn't...but I want to so badly... Her brain tornado whirled, the conflicting thoughts tossed about by a force that felt out of her control.

The only clear thought she had was: find Charlie *immediately*.

"Breathe in...breathe out," Charlie coached a hyperventilating Emma a few minutes later. He pushed her toward a chair near the administrative offices and sat down beside her. "It's all good. *Really* good."

But Emma wasn't convinced. This wasn't some little white lie. This wasn't pretending to like Holly's unfortunate new haircut or telling her mom she would clean her room tonight. This was pretending to be someone else on the pages of the country's biggest fashion magazine. And she didn't need psychic powers to know that if Paige found out she was being tricked, it wouldn't end well.

"Hi, guys." Emma's mom appeared in front of them, the door to the admin offices closing behind her. Her smile quickly faded into concern. "Emma, is everything all right? You don't look so good. A little white, actually." Joan put the back of her hand against Emma's clammy forehead. "Are you here to see the nurse?"

"No!" Emma blurted, more forcefully than obviously necessary. "I mean, I'm not here for the nurse. I…um…" Emma fumbled, pleading with her eyes for Charlie to do what he did best. Talk his way out.

"Emma's just in shock because, uh, she just got an A on a pop quiz in bio," Charlie offered.

"Really? Way to go, Em!" her mother said. "Now, if you just focus your energies like that on the Western civ exam, you'll ace that too."

That's what he came up with? Why doesn't he dig a hole and bury me now?

Emma smiled weakly at her mother.

"Well, got to run to class," her mother said. "Which is probably what you two should be doing now, too. Right?"

Charlie scrambled to his feet and dragged Emma up with him. "On our way!"

Emma's mom waved good-bye before heading off in the other direction. Emma watched her mom leave and had the sudden feeling she was in a *What Not to Wear* episode, featuring Joan Rose. She was about to protest her mom's scuffed clogs when she noticed that Charlie's usual smirk had suddenly turned serious.

"You can't fess up now," he lectured Emma, pulling her behind the stairwell. "This is your big break—the biggest! It's one of those once-in-a-lifetime things."

"But, what about—"

"You can't freak out. I have a plan—well, sort of. Listen, you design, and I'll run everything else. It's going to be awesome. You can do this, Em. And you should."

Emma thought back to all the happy designing daydreams she'd had during class. "I should, shouldn't I?" she echoed, the conviction growing in her voice. Having Allegra's clothes photographed for the magazine would get *her* that much closer to all her dreams and maybe even more. "I mean, it'd be silly to turn down this opportunity, right? Who knows when—or *if*—it will happen again."

Emma pulled out her cell, and together they composed a very different message than she would've just ten minutes earlier.

> Ms. Young: Wld b honored 2 provide my designs 4 the photo shoot. Pls let me know what u need 2 make the shoot happen. All best, AB

Emma felt herself drifting that afternoon, mentally afloat, as she sketched madly in the margins of her world history notebook. Sheer, flowing tunics. A braided vine-like belt. Ms. Lyons's words on Athens and ancient Greece flicked in and out, background noise serving only to add to design inspiration. A toga dress with gladiator sandals.

Suddenly, she noticed Jackson Creedon looking at her

across the classroom with a strange expression on his face. She bolted to attention. Why is Jackson looking at me? He *never* looks at me! Then it hit her. She had been staring at him for the last five—God, was it ten?—minutes without even knowing it.

Her eyes grew wide. This was beyond mortifying. She quickly lurched back in her chair, pulling her textbook up to mask her face, which felt as if she'd baked it in the oven. Her hot pink hoodie knocked the strap from her messenger bag, and, as if in slow motion, the bag slid off the back of her chair. She lunged to catch it.

Too late! Fashion magazines flagged with dozens of Post-It Notes spilled out around her chair. A dozen random antique-coin buttons clanked and skittered in all directions across the linoleum floor. But worst of all, her sketchbook landed spine down, open to the page of Jackson in her redesigned soccer uniform.

The teacher stopped talking. Emma could feel everyone's eyes on her. She had to get that sketchbook before Jackson—or anyone else—saw her drawings!

Emma hurled herself to the floor. She dove for her sketchbook and slapped it shut, shoving it deep inside the bag.

Crawling on hands and knees, she grabbed at buttons right and left. Out of the corner of her eye, she noticed something shiny near Jackson's sneaker. A button. One of her buttons was sitting inches away from his foot! There's no way I'm going over there, she vowed as she scrambled around scooping up the other buttons.

Finally she had all but one of them clutched in her fists. She spun around to clamber back to her desk. Just then, a closed hand thrust toward her and slowly opened to reveal the renegade button. It was Jackson's hand. He carefully placed the shiny silver button in her open palm. It was still warm from his touch.

"Thanks," Emma said. As she stood up, she sneaked a peek at his face. Maybe it was the post-traumatic stress of the whole embarrassing incident distorting her vision, but maybe—just maybe—she wasn't imagining that Jackson was smiling at her.

She tucked the Jackson button into a small zipped pocket of her messenger bag for safekeeping. If she was ever going to use it, it would be on something super-special.

Emma jogged up the subway stairs and inhaled deeply when she reached the street. The sun was shining; the sky was azure blue; the air was crisp; the boy she liked had smiled at her and she had a button to prove it…and the stoplight was red, meaning that she could cross 34th Street. What a great day, she thought, practically skipping across the crosswalk and dancing around people who didn't seem to notice or appreciate the amazing-ness of the afternoon. She leaped onto the curb and strolled up Fashion Avenue, humming and smiling.

Then her cell buzzed with a new text.

> Ms. Biscotti: I need 3 brand-new pieces 4 Spring season @ Madison offices by Mon 11/2 4 the photo shoot. Pls confirm that's doable 4 u. Thx. Ciao, Paige Young

Emma stopped, confused. Three new pieces…for the spring season?

Minutes later, she sprinted back to her studio, barely waving to Marjorie. She threw down her school bag and lunged for the garment rack where her finished—or in some cases, temporarily abandoned—designs hung.

Let's see. There must be something here I could use that would be right for spring, Emma thought. She was much more adventurous with her original fashion designs than with the outfits she wore to school. It was easier to design for fantasy people whose lives were definitely far more exciting, dynamic, and glamorous than hers.

The two dresses she just finished were on the front of the rack. Too bad Paige had seen them already and now owned

one that looked a lot like the pineapple-colored dress because they would've been perfect.

She loved the off-white cotton-linen corset dress she'd made during the summer, but somehow it didn't feel special enough for *Madison*. The dusty rose and white geometric-print silk jersey dress would've been great, but she messed up the ruching big time. It was all bunched up and uneven in the back. There was no fixing that.

She could try finishing the fire-engine red coat that she constructed with her grandmother last spring, but hand-sewing all that embroidery on the collar and oversized cuffs could take two weeks alone. The only other thing she had was a Chanel-like sheath dress, but she'd made it in black wool tweed. Hardly springy.

The truth suddenly became crystal clear.

I'm going to have to make three new pieces…from scratch.

After dinner that night, Emma sat on her bed, surveying the chaos she had created. She'd ransacked her room

looking for design ideas in every old sketchbook. Thousands of sketches, and nothing seemed cutting edge enough. She flipped through her work again. Party dresses with flirty hems and playful beadwork. Leather pants that fit like a second skin. Short skirts with hundreds of pleats. Long, flowy tunics with funky necklines.

Do I even know how to make half of this stuff? she wondered. *Sketching is one thing. Constructing a few cute dresses is still basically one thing. But three perfectly finished pieces that work together like they're part of a collection? How am I going to pull that off—alone and in two weeks?*

Emma's bedroom door swung open. William.

"What happened to your hand? Forget how to knock?" Emma said. Honestly, she didn't know whether she was annoyed that he had interrupted her…or the teeniest bit relieved to have the unexpected distraction.

"Why should I bother knocking? It's not like you'd let me in anyway," William replied with a shrug.

"True but *so* not the point," Emma warned. She was just about to kick him out when she had an idea. "Hey, since you're here, maybe you could make yourself useful."

William's face lit up. "Really? I mean, sure, whatever."

"Come in and sit." She cleared off a tiny spot for him to perch at the end of her bed. Emma held up sketches of two different dresses to show William: one a fuchsia strapless tiered-ruffle mini, and the other a long-sleeved subtle A-line black one with leopard-print collar, cuffs, and pockets. "Which one do you like better: this one or this one?"

He scrunched up his face and then pointed to the strapless mini.

"Hmm. Okay, good." She put down those sketchbooks and picked up two more, flipping to a drawing of an updated opera coat with three-quarter-length sleeves and big rhinestone buttons and shimmery trim, and another of a short-cropped gold jacket with bracelet-length sleeves and graffiti-like multicolored embroidery on the back. "This one or that one?"

"That one!" he said more enthusiastically this time, tapping the sketch of the cropped jacket with his fingers.

"All right…" Emma shuffled sketchbooks again and held up two more. "How about this"—swingy, wide-legged raw silk trousers in a cobalt blue—"or this?"—black satin skinny pants with zippers and studs and a baby-pink silk ribbon belt.

"This one!" He pointed at the wide-legged trousers, bouncing up and down on the bed.

Hey, this is actually good, Emma thought. He was helping narrow down some of her options.

"Now let's go back to the beginning," she said, reaching for the first sketches she showed him. "Why did you choose the strapless minidress over the leopard-print one?"

He blinked at her a few times.

"You don't have to use any fancy fashion terms," she explained. "Just tell me what you like about this dress in your own words. The color? The shape? A certain detail?"

"I didn't know I was supposed to have a reason." He shrugged and smirked. "I just kept going back and forth between what was in your left hand and what was in your right."

"Out!" Emma screamed. She couldn't believe he lured her into his little game. "Get out of here."

Will danced a victory dance, a cross between a winning-touchdown celebration and the jig of the Lucky Charms guy. "Already gone." He flashed a satisfied smile as he left the room.

Emma flopped back against her pillows, spreading her arms wide. She imagined herself in a charming design studio in Paris—black-and-white toile wallpaper and hot-pink velvet sofas—a place where fashionable ideas flowed. Not in a messy apartment with an annoying brother. But that wasn't going to happen. At least not tonight.

I need ideas that are striking, she thought, things that will put Allegra Biscotti on the fashion map. Her designs had to live up to what Paige said in her blog about Allegra's designs being "fresh," "playful," and "imaginative."

It was weird. She'd never thought that she was designing the way Paige Young had said. She just designed what she wanted from things she saw that inspired her, made her curious, or—like when she played the Game—made her want to redo something *her* way. Sometimes she just fell in love with a fabric or a color—or a button made of dozens of tiny pink and red rhinestones. It was never a conscious thing. Her designs just sort of happened.

She hated feeling like this, so unsure, so nervous.

She raised her head. I *never* feel like that when I'm making things for myself, she realized. I need to concentrate on what *I* think, what *I* like, what makes *me* happy.

She was determined to come up with something—something that would be *fun* to create.

NIGHT BELOW THE SURFACE

The usual amount of school-assembly chaos greeted Emma as she walked into the auditorium for last period. All the students, as well as the whole faculty and most of the staff, were packed into the room, and everyone seemed be taking full advantage of the minutes before the program started—something about a new eco-friendly initiative Downtown Day was launching—to socialize at top volume.

Two days had passed since Paige had asked Allegra for clothes for the photo shoot, and Emma still hadn't come up with any fabulous fashion-forward ideas. Not even any semi-fabulous ones.

Emma scanned the crowd looking for Holly. Holly had texted her that morning, saying Emma should sit with *her*—not *us*. Emma wondered if that was her way of apologizing for the Bloomingdale's Incident. She hoped so. She could use some friendship repair time, just her and Holly.

She spotted the back of Holly's head about halfway down the aisle and hurried toward her. She stopped when she saw Ivana's trademark red hair. Holly sat next to Ivana. And Lexie, Shannon, and Kayla. *Unreal*, Emma thought, trying to figure out what Holly was up to. There was no seat for her.

Why did Holly bother asking me to sit next to her if she was just going to sit with them? Emma wondered. She shifted on her feet, not knowing where to go. Somehow she was the only one standing in the aisle. Everyone else was already slumped in a seat.

Emma felt her confusion harden, tighten into anger.

"Holly," she called through gritted teeth. "Holly!"

Holly finally turned and waved. As if nothing was wrong. Emma tried to call up the nerve to just walk away. To leave Holly. Instead, she stood, frozen in the aisle, completely awkward, as she waited for Holly to scurry across the row.

"Sorry, Em. The seat thing kind of just...happened," Holly whispered, anxiously glancing over toward Ivana and the 'Bees to see if they were watching her.

She's actually nervous to be seen talking to me? The sitting-together thing was her idea. And now there's nowhere for me to sit at all. Emma wasn't sure what she was supposed to do. Mean-girl comebacks weren't her thing. She could never achieve the right withering tone and stance. But she either had to let Holly have it or walk away or—

"Oops! I left my bag over there by mistake," Holly said strangely loudly as she walked a few rows back. She reached across a couple of seats and plucked her bag off an empty chair. Then she motioned Emma. "Em, you should sit here."

Emma so wanted to tell Holly where *she* should sit. Then Emma saw the seat Holly was pointing to. It was right next to Jackson.

"Two-minute warning, people!" Vice Principal Manning's voice boomed over the loudspeakers. "Please start settling down. We're going to start as soon as we get our video equipment running."

Emma glanced around quickly. Every seat in this part of the auditorium was taken. Except that one. Jackson was too busy reading a book to notice that she and Holly were even standing there. What if Jackson is saving this seat for someone else...like Lexie? But no, Lexie was in her rightful place on the other side of Ivana.

Holly nudged her with her foot and nodded, then hurried back to her own spot.

Emma felt her feet carrying her toward Jackson before her brain could formulate a plan. She gingerly slid into the maroon fabric seat next to him. Had Holly been planning for Emma to sit next to Jackson all along? Was this Holly's wacky way of making up? Emma considered the possibilities as the vice principal and some other staff members huddled around the tech table. They didn't seem to be making much progress.

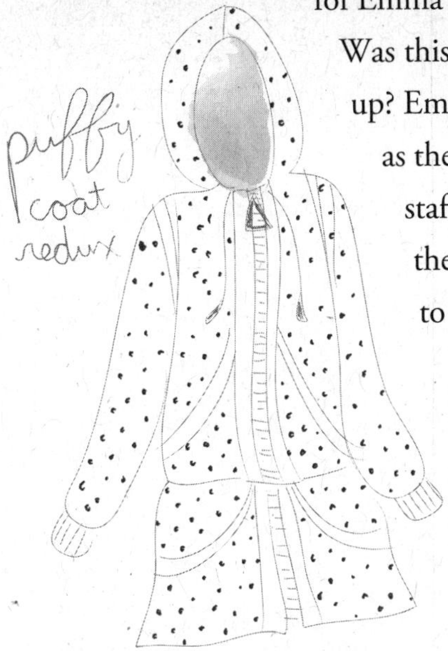

She finally let herself glance quickly to the left. That's not the inside of a biology book, Emma thought. She craned her neck to get a better peek. Now she could see exactly what he was so interested in. A comic book hidden inside the textbook. A second later, Clayton Vanderbeck, one of the guys on the soccer team, reached across Emma from behind and snatched the comic out of Jackson's hands.

"Hey, give it back, Vanderbeck!" Jackson demanded.

"No way, dude!" Clayton replied.

Emma noticed Lexie twisting around to see what was going on behind her. She watched as Lexie's eyes shifted from Jackson to Emma sitting beside him and back to Jackson again. She whipped around to whisper something to Ivana. Then the two of them turned to look. Emma slid down in

puffy coat redux

her seat to avoid two sets of icy stares. Will they please start the stupid assembly already?

"Come on, Clay," Jackson said. "You can have it when I'm done."

"No, you can have it when *I'm* done," Clayton quipped, settling himself comfortably in his chair and opening the stolen book to the first page.

Jackson grumbled something under his breath. His leg bounced up and down as he patted his thigh with his hand. Emma didn't dare look over, but she bet he was biting his lip. Without warning, Jackson lunged across Emma to grab his book back from Clayton.

The edge of his forest-green shirt brushed her cheek, and she got a faint whiff of something that smelled unfamiliar yet pleasant. It took her a second to realize that the scent came from Jackson. The part of Emma's face where his shirt had touched suddenly tingled. Now she had another Real Jackson detail to add to her slowly growing inventory: Jackson smelled awesome!

"Sorry 'bout that," Jackson said.

Shocked by the sound of his voice, Emma glanced at him. He wasn't looking at her, so she wasn't one hundred percent sure he was even speaking to her.

"No worries," she croaked.

"Did you finish your world history paper yet?" he asked, his face buried in his comic book.

"Sort of," she said. Then she panicked. That sounded like she was ending the conversation. That was the last thing she wanted. So she quickly added, "I'm probably about halfway through. I need to finish it tonight since it's due tomorrow."

"Yeah, me, too."

Now what? Emma wondered. She focused her eyes on the comic book. "What are you reading, I mean, instead of studying for bio?"

Jackson finally looked at her with his sky-blue eyes, sending an electric current through Emma. He reached across with his left hand to rake his brown wavy hair away from his face, but it just flopped forward again, covering his right eye.

"It's a graphic novel called *Night below the Surface.*" Despite the ruckus of the auditorium, his voice was soft and low, as if he were sharing a very special secret only with Emma. "It's kind of a series. I'm pretty into it. This is the second one—it just came out."

Emma could hardly believe she was having a real live conversation with Jackson. She had to keep it going as long as possible. Who knew when an opportunity like this would come up again?

"Sounds interesting. Can I see?"

"Sure." He handed it to her. "You into graphic novels?"

"No—well, not yet." Emma flipped through the pages. The illustrations were in black, white, and charcoal gray with touches of various shades of blue and yellow here and there... they were dark and dramatic but beautiful. "What's it about?"

Jackson shifted around to lean forward on the armrest between them to get a better view of the pages. They weren't touching, but they were close enough—the closest she had ever been to him—to make Emma's heart start pounding wildly, maybe even loudly enough for him to hear. Luckily, the noise level in the auditorium was still pretty high.

"It's about this group of teens who were the only survivors of the apocalypse," he explained. "They started their own society, but they have to live underground in this urban jungle to stay hidden away from the forces of evil roaming the surface.

"See those two? They're the main characters—a brother and a sister. They're kind of the leaders. His best friend also survived, but we're not sure yet if he's still a good guy or if he became a bad guy in the last book. But he's definitely hiding *something*—we just don't know what yet."

"Wow," Emma said. "That sounds really cool." And a lot like what's going on in my life. As she turned the pages, she felt herself being drawn more deeply into the story—not by the text but by the moody illustrations of this mysterious underground world. She couldn't get enough of the characters' sleek, futuristic clothes, especially the sister-leader. She was beautiful and strong and fierce. Emma was dying to hear more—both of the story *and* Jackson's voice—but just then Vice Principal Manning tapped loudly on the microphone, making everyone jump.

The magic moment was gone…

Emma handed the book to Jackson. As he tucked it back into his textbook, Emma caught Lexie turning around again to check up on the Jackson situation. But this time Emma did not hide. She deep down actually hoped Lexie had seen Jackson talking to her and showing her the book.

"Hello!" Vice Principal Manning said. "Hi, okay, we're ready to get started here. Sorry for the delay, everyone. Technical difficulties!"

As soon as the assembly was over, Jackson was out of his seat, joining his soccer team friends already making their way up the aisle. Emma's heart still beat like crazy from both the excitement of sitting next to him for thirty whole minutes *and* because now she had a fantastic idea for her designs for *Madison* magazine.

Holly sidled up next to her. Emma totally expected to see Ivana and the 'Bees right behind Holly, but they were nowhere to be found. They must've ducked out a side exit. She smiled at Holly. Maybe things were back to normal with them. Maybe her friendship with Ivana was a passing fad—like Crocs or neon clothes—whose time had faded.

"So how'd it go?" Holly asked eagerly.

"Actually…it was awesome." Emma beamed. "I promise I'll tell you all about it, but I've got to go. I'll call you later, okay?" Emma hurried toward the exit. There was no time to waste. She had to get started on her designs. They were going to be like nothing she had ever done before. It was a good thing Holly hadn't saved her a seat!

THE ALLURE OF ALLURE

Into post-apocalyptic graphic novels these days, Em?" Charlie asked as he entered Emma's work space at Laceland the next afternoon. He nodded at her inspiration wall, now covered in pages from *Night below the Surface*.

Since the second *Night below the Surface* book—the one that Jackson was reading—had just come out only a few days before, Emma had to go to three bookstores before she could track down a copy for herself. She'd spent all of the night before flagging her favorite pages and sketching madly. She hadn't even taken her homework out of her bag.

"Not really," Emma replied. "Just this series. I saw, um, a boy at school reading it, and I thought it might be good as inspiration for Allegra's collection. It's cool, right?"

Charlie walked along the wall, looking at the different illustrations Emma had cut out. "So Allegra is going to be making futuristic clothes that could survive the end of our civilization as we know it?"

"Nope. I mean, the clothes are cool and everything, but

I don't think futuristic is really Allegra's thing," Emma explained. "Besides, she needs to make them her own—interpret them in her own way—not just make designs that another artist came up with, you know? That would be like, too literal...and not particularly creative."

Charlie settled himself on the stool across the table from Emma. "I get it. So what do you and Allegra have in mind?"

"Do you know what the book's about?" Emma asked.

"I read the first one. But it looks like I won't be able to borrow the second one from you." Charlie picked the shredded remains of *NBTS 2* off Emma's worktable. Emma had cut out full pages in some places and smaller frames in others.

"When I first heard what the story was about, I was caught up in the idea of hiding. The main characters have to hide from the evil forces, so they can't live freely or be who they really are. Which I can really relate to right now."

She smiled at Charlie—the only one who was in on her "double life." Charlie might just be the only person she wasn't hiding *anything* from—except for that crush on Jackson...

"Anyhow," she continued, "I'm going to design three pieces, all with amazing linings somewhere inside. I just love the idea of giving people a peek of hem or a pocket lining or the inside of a cuff or collar and revealing something secret and special on the inside. And I'm going to do it all in the same colors as in *Night below the Surface*."

"That sounds seriously cool," Charlie said appreciatively. "Very Allegra Biscotti. Let me see the sketches."

"They're still totally in progress." She slid her sketchbook across the table and pointed. "That sketch and two on the next page."

The first design was of an iridescent, stretchy silvery dress that ended just below the knee and had a side slit to mid-thigh. It had a deep neckline with a short, stand-up collar like the ones on the Chinese silk jackets hanging from all of the stalls in Chinatown. The slit and inside of the collar would offer a peek at a pretty print lining of some sort. Emma was also planning to use the lining fabric on one side of the belt, so that it could be tied at the waist with either the print or the solid dress fabric facing out.

The next was a charcoal-gray, three-quarter-sleeve jacket with an exaggerated high collar and wide, swingy bottom with a box pleat in the back. Emma planned to line the inside of the collar, the turned-up cuffs, and the inside of the box pleat with a different printed fabric. If she had time, she might try to make gloves out of the lining fabric, too.

Her third piece was a dove-gray fitted vest with several patch and welt pockets—some of them hidden inside—that could be worn alone, with either of the two other pieces, or anything else, like a white T-shirt or blouse. She'd have to find a fabric with a lot of stretch because she wanted the vest to be super-fitted. It would also be fully lined with yet another splendid print.

"So what's next?" Charlie asked, genuinely curious.

"Next I have to sketch out every piece of each garment from every view—you know, from the front, back, and sides. Those sketches are called 'flats,' because they're flat-line drawings without any color. On those I need to put in all the details like how many buttons and buttonholes I need, where a zipper or pockets should go, how the collar and cuffs should work, darts, seaming—technical stuff like that. And then I drape muslin onto the dress forms to figure out the size and shape of each piece."

"Muslin?"

"Yeah. It's this white cotton fabric. Way cheap, so my mistakes aren't expensive mistakes. My grandma taught me to use it. Then I start making my patterns."

"Whoa. That's too much work. Can't you just get the material and sew?" Charlie asked.

Emma laughed. "No. Then you end up with an ugly mess. Mismatched sleeves, crooked seams..."

"You're right." Charlie nodded. "No 'Intro to Sewing' projects here. This is the real deal. *Madison* mag."

"Shoot!" she said, noticing the time, "I want to go to the fabric store before it closes. I need to see the kinds of fabrics I can afford, so I can work them into the designs."

Charlie reached into his backpack, pulled out a crumpled white envelope, and slid it across the worktable toward Emma.

"What's this?"

"Open it. It's for you."

Emma peeled the flap and peered inside. Money. Several twenties, fives, and ones bundled together with a rubber band.

Emma could not imagine what this was for. Or where Charlie had gotten it.

"Why are you paying me?"

"I'm not. I'm *contributing*," Charlie explained.

"Contributing to what?"

Charlie let out an exasperated sigh. "Look, Em. I may act like an idiot sometimes, but I'm really not. I know that making clothes, clothes that are hot enough to make it onto the pages of *Madison*, costs money. And I know that you can't possibly have the cash to afford the fabric you want without hitting up your parents, which I know there's no chance of, so here. It's not a lot, but it's something."

Emma fingered the worn bills. The right thing, the thing her mother had trained her to do, would be to give the money back to Charlie. But she could so use the extra cash. As it was, she was going to have to empty her entire sock-drawer cash stash. She had even debated the pros and cons of pleading with William for money.

"But, Charlie—" She'd never taken money from a friend before.

"Look. It's not a gift. Does that make you feel better? It's a loan. Like in the theater, people put up money to help get a show on Broadway. Then when the show's a hit, they get their money back plus a little extra. Trust me, I'll be collecting when everyone lines up to buy your clothes." Charlie was back to being Charlie. And Emma knew he would come collecting, which was strangely comforting.

"Thanks," Emma replied. Now they really were in this together. "Want to come to the fabric store with me?"

"Nah. I'll just hang here."

"Don't think you can." Emma gathered up her sketchbook, pencils, and markers. "I'm not coming back. I have to finish a world history paper, which is late, and read a zillion chapters of *A Separate Peace* tonight."

"If you don't have time for me now," Charlie teased, "what happens when you become über-successful?"

"Don't worry," Emma replied, turning off the light above her worktable. "Allegra will always remember the little people who helped her get where she is..."

"Which is...middle school?" Charlie guessed, following her down the dark hall.

"Yup. And unless she gets that history paper done, she may not even be there!"

After Charlie headed home toward the prospect of five wannabe actresses singing songs from *Wicked* in his apartment, Emma walked the six blocks to Allure Fabrics.

Even though it was late in the day, Allure was crawling with students from the Fashion Institute of Technology. With thousands of bolts of fabrics piled on shelves that reached all the way to the ceiling, the store's acoustics completely muted the sound of their excited chatter.

Allure Fabrics was one of Emma's favorite places. For the past two years, since she'd been allowed to wander around New York City on her own, every time she walked into Allure, she got the same rush as she did as a little girl going into Economy Candy, the lower Eastside sweets emporium. Only now bold graphic prints, shimmery gem-colored satins, nubby Easter-egg-colored tweeds, and butter-soft jerseys made her heart race instead of bins full of gumballs, jellybeans, and chocolate marshmallow twists.

She loved how the fabrics were grouped by colors, textures, patterns, and weights. Chiffon. Denim. Duchess satin. Eyelet. Linen. Twill. Tulle. Velvet. Every kind of silk imaginable, from batiste to voile. Even organic cotton and eco-friendly fabric made from bamboo. It amazed her how many different possibilities there were—and slight variations within those themes—and yet somehow, there was an order to them.

Sometimes she would come here and just follow the fashion students up and down the aisles as they selected material for school projects. But today Emma was on her own mission. And for that, she needed Nidhi.

Nidhi was Emma's favorite salesperson at Allure. She was in her late twenties, fashionable and funky—and a little quirky, which made Emma love her even more. Her midnight-black hair was pin-straight and cut into a choppy fringe that framed her face. She was only a little taller than Emma, but her confidence—and high heels—made her tower over Emma in her flats. Nidhi worked part time at Allure to make money and industry connections until she could get her own clothing line together. Plus the employee discount on fabrics helped her afford to design her own things.

Emma walked back into the depths of the cavernous store. A swarm of students surrounded Nidhi, fighting one another for her attention.

"I saw it first, Lila!"

"You are so lying, Crystal!" Lila retorted, clutching a bolt of purple, red, and yellow charmeuse. "I found this like twenty minutes ago!"

"But then you put it back, so it's fair game!" Crystal screeched

"Ladies!" Nidhi shouted as best she could with her naturally quiet voice. "This fabric comes in more than one color, so you can both have it. Or not. Flip a coin or draw straws or something. Then let me know when you decide. I have other customers, yeah?"

Nidhi wriggled out from between them and practically fell onto Emma in relief. "Hi cutie! Sorry about that. First years—always the same. Zillions of fabrics to choose from, and everyone wants the same one! Never fails." She threw up her hands. "What're you looking for today? I don't have anything new on sale yet. Maybe next week."

"Actually," Emma said, "this time I may buy some things at full price."

Nidhi grabbed her chest as if she were having a heart attack, jingling the array of tiny gold charms that dangled from her triple-strand necklace. "No! It can't be! My best bargain hunter paying full retail? What's the occasion? Making a dress for some dance at that fancy school you go to?"

Emma snorted and waved her hand. "Hardly. But it *is* a special occasion."

"Good enough for me, yeah? Tell me what you need."

Nidhi's eyes jumped from Emma's face to something going on over her shoulder. "I have to go break up another fight. Go look on that table—we just got in new stuff."

As Nidhi marched away on her suede wedges, Emma hurried over to the new arrivals table. She was immediately drawn to a bolt of silk covered in a watercolor design boasting many of the same hues—cobalt and turquoise and other aquatic shades—as in *Night below the Surface*. There wasn't much left, but she could probably make it work somewhere.

Before Emma could reach for the bolt, a take-no-prisoners fashion design student with wildly curly brown hair appeared out of nowhere. She snatched it off the table. Emma noticed her fingers were covered with dozens of mermaid-shaped silver rings.

"Excuse me. I…I was looking at that one," Emma stammered. "Are you going to buy all of it?"

"Probably," she sneered, tucking the fabric roll under her arm and striding toward the cash registers in lace-up green combat boots.

I should've grabbed it when I saw it, Emma thought, angry with herself. She

sized up the fabric thief. No question about it. She was much bigger and meaner looking than Emma. Plus the tips of all those mini-mermaid fins look pointy and sharp and way dangerous. Emma had no chance of grabbing the fabric back.

"Store closing in twenty minutes! *Twenty* minutes! No exceptions! I don't care if your professor gives you an F or you cry real tears!" Abe Sherman, the gruff and grumpy owner of Allure, shouted. He was famous for his permanent bad mood. Emma suspected it was all an act, but she kept a healthy distance all the same.

"Okay, I'm back," Nidhi said as she walked up to Emma. "Quick—tell me."

Emma explained that she needed three shades of gray that worked together—an iridescent silver, something charcoal, and a lighter dove gray. She wanted all of the textures to be

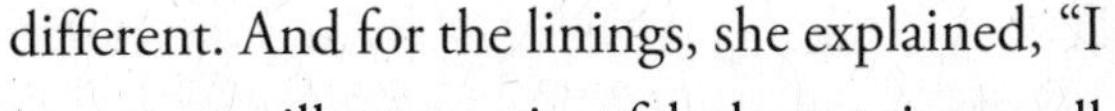

different. And for the linings, she explained, "I want silky or satiny fabulous prints—all different kinds—with cobalt, turquoise, and canary yellow. And they all need to work together somehow. I saw one on the new arrivals table, but—"

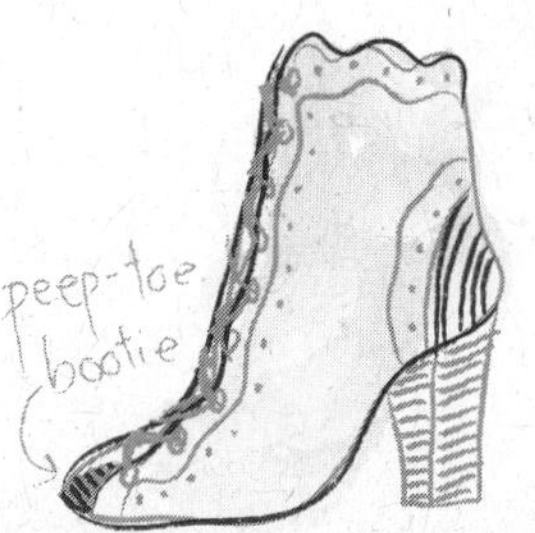

Before Emma had even finished, Nidhi was off and running. Emma had to speed-walk to keep up even though Emma was running around in silver Converse sneakers and Nidhi was tottering on mountainous wedges. Nidhi darted through the store, her head snapping up and down as she expertly scanned the shelves.

When her arms were full, she dropped off an ocean of deep blue, bright turquoise, and hot yellow prints on an empty cutting table and then did another circuit collecting bolts of gray, which she deposited onto the same table. Emma's hand immediately reached for a glossy satin in a watercolor blue print that was similar to the one she had seen—and lost—on the new arrivals table.

"This one's a blend, so it's much cheaper than that other one that the crazy-haired hyena stole out from under you," Nidhi said with a wink. "But it's great quality—from one of our best suppliers. I didn't show the other girl. I'd much rather get you the better bargain. What else?"

"I love this one, too," Emma said pointing to a wild, Pucci-esque swirl in the gray and yellow tones from her color scheme. She rubbed the heavy silk shantung against the inside of her arm, and it sent shivers to her neck.

"And this!" She ran her hands over a pleated silk charmeuse with narrow, uneven stripes in the same cobalt blue and canary yellow mixed with gray and creamy white.

She then turned her attention to the gray pile, which was all about texture. Everything Nidhi had pulled hit the mark in terms of color and quality, so it was a matter of pulling three fabrics that played off one another.

For the dress, she chose slate gray chiffon with micro sequins. She was nervous about working with the fabric—it seemed so delicate. But it was *so* right! For the jacket, she fell in love with a charcoal-gray jacquard in a heavy but soft cotton rip-stop. For the vest, she unrolled four different dove-colored silk jersey knits and chose the one with the most stretch.

"They're all perfect, Nidhi," Emma gushed.

"Of course. I always find you what you need, yeah?" She looked pleased with herself. "How much do you want? Quick, quick, before Abe starts yelling again. I have such a headache today. Mid-terms coming up over at the design school. My least favorite times of year."

Emma bit her lip. "I don't know…yet. I still have to make my patterns and figure out how much I need. But I definitely want these. I just can't buy them…today."

Nidhi smiled knowingly. She was always patient with Emma, probably because Emma tried very hard never to waste Nidhi's time or drive her crazy—unlike the design students. "I'll put these on hold as long as you promise not to tell Abe. When will you come back? Saturday, yeah?"

"Yes. Definitely Saturday!"

"Wow, that's going to be a pretty big purchase." Nidhi's dark eyes glinted at Emma.

"My biggest, for sure." Emma had already done the math in her head. She turned, then hesitated. She hated leaving the lining fabric behind. She wanted to feel the material and mix and match the linings with the outer fabrics as her designs took shape. "Could I possibly get a tiny swatch of each of these?"

In one swift motion, Nidhi pulled a pair of fabric shears from a sheath clipped to the waistband of her short camel-wool wrap skirt and snipped little triangles off each bolt. With a cupped hand, she swept them off the cutting table and slipped them into Emma's palm.

As Emma wound her way back to the front of the store, a wave of excitement washed over her. Deep in the pocket of her mocha-brown velvet trench, her fingers lightly danced over the small yet precious pieces of fabric. They were the beginning. The beginning of her first collection.

The first-ever Allegra Biscotti collection.

DESIGNER 2 WATCH

"I made you a schedule," Charlie announced at Emma's locker Monday morning.

"Seriously?"

"Yeah." Charlie, who never got embarrassed, looked slightly uncomfortable as he handed her a chart printed out from his computer. "It's nothing major. Just a calendar showing how many days left and when each piece should be finished."

"It doesn't work like that," Emma said. "It's not like I finish one piece and then start another. They all kind of flow together."

"Fine, so toss it." Charlie reached for his chart, but Emma held tight and pushed it into her locker. When her mother constantly followed up on her schoolwork, Emma found herself unendingly frustrated. But having Charlie check up on her was a nice surprise.

On Friday, Emma had run directly from school to buy the muslin. She'd spent the entire weekend working on her collection—first draping the dress forms at her studio; then creating the patterns; then mixing and matching. After much pinning and unpinning of the tiny swatches, she was able to buy the right amount of fabric. Naturally, she'd holed up in her bedroom into the night cutting the fabric with her favorite fabric shears—which meant she was more exhausted than usual for a Monday morning.

"The only thing I didn't get to do was homework," Emma admitted to Charlie. "But I have a plan for that. I'll squeeze it all in during study hall and lunch this week."

It wasn't like she loved sitting with Ivana and the 'Bees in the cafeteria anyway. Emma figured they probably wouldn't even notice that she was gone. As for Holly, Emma wasn't sure if the peace offering in the auditorium was just a one-time thing. She was beginning to suspect not having Emma around made Holly's life with her new friends much simpler.

"Any chance you're ready for the geometry quiz this morning?"

Emma stared at Charlie. "What quiz? Oh, no. I totally forgot." She scrambled to find her math textbook. Maybe if she glanced at the problems right now, she'd luck out and pull off a C on that one.

"Bees at three o'clock," Charlie mumbled out of the side of his mouth. He nodded toward Lexie and Kayla, who were now standing at the other end of the hall.

Emma's mouth dropped open.

"What?" Charlie asked.

"I…can't believe it!" Emma gasped, peering around Charlie's shoulder. "Lexie is wearing the exact same outfit I styled for Holly at Bloomingdale's. Well, she switched the pink sequined miniskirt for a pink corduroy one, but otherwise it's the same!"

"The one you told me they busted on?" Charlie asked, trying to take a peek without being obvious.

"Yes! Tell me what they're doing," Emma demanded.

"Holly, Ivana, and Shannon are with them now," he reported. "And Lexie is spinning around, like she's showing them her outfit."

Emma could hear the girls—especially the famously loud Ivana—oohing and ahhing over Lexie's outfit, *Emma's* outfit, all the way down the hall. She doubted that any of them was giving her a single ounce of credit. Emma stood on tiptoes to sneak a look over Charlie's shoulder again. She had to admit Lexie looked pretty fabulous. The gray mohair sweater-vest made her long dark hair look that much shinier, and the miniskirt showed off her tanned, athletic legs.

"Ugh—here they come," Emma said, sinking back on her feet.

"Later!" Charlie said. He took off in the opposite direction.

"Coward!" Emma loudly whispered after him.

Moments later, the girls crowded around Holly's locker.

"Hi, Em," Holly said. The other girls stood talking and giggling behind her, waiting for her to grab her books.

"Hey," Emma replied. "Sorry, but I'm not going to be at lunch today. I need to go to the library."

Holly popped a bubble and shrugged. "No biggie. You ready for the geometry quiz? I think it's going to be kind of hard."

"Uh, no. Not really," Emma answered. *How can Holly just stand there and pretend like this isn't the most awkward moment ever?* Emma wondered. *She must realize that Lexie took my outfit combination, since Holly was the one who wore it first.*

"Cute outfit, Lexie," Emma ventured, hoping her subtle comment might prompt Holly to acknowledge the truth. "Really cool combo."

the REAL winner!

Emma waited for Holly's reaction. But she didn't have one. Holly just continued pulling stuff out of the locker, getting ready for the first few periods of the day.

"Thanks." Lexie beamed with genuine delight. "It's my new favorite. Fun, isn't it?"

"Super-fun," Emma responded sarcastically. "It kind of looks like the one I styled in Bloomie's, don't you think?" She spoke to Lexie but stared directly at Holly.

"Not at all." Ivana quickly jumped to her friend's defense. "This outfit is much more stylish."

Emma continued to stare at Holly. Willing her to say something. But Holly remained mute, suddenly intent on organizing pens and pencils in a case.

Emma glanced down at the geometry book in her hand, then over at Lexie's outfit and Holly fervently lining up pencils. So this was how it was going to be. She slammed her locker shut and walked away.

She wondered if Coco Chanel had days like these.

Six hours later, as Emma pushed down on the foot pedal of her sewing machine, laying down the first stitches to the Allegra Biscotti Collection, thoughts of her so-called best friend and quizzes on congruent triangles were blissfully forgotten. She began with the jacket, joining each piece together—left side front to left side back, right side front to right side back—with flawless seams.

She had sewn something so structured only a couple of times before, and that had been with her grandmother sitting right next to her, coaching her like an air-traffic controller guiding in

a plane. Step by step. I hope I can remember all the tricks Grandma Grace taught me, Emma thought as she worked two sleeve pieces together under the bobbing silver needle.

Emma studied the newly sewn sleeve and the open armhole. Attaching the sleeve correctly was the trickiest part. Her hands began to flutter. If I measured and cut the patterns right, the sleeve should fit perfectly. But by the time she had re-threaded the machine, her hands were trembling.

How she wished her grandmother was here beside her—or at least in her condo in Florida. Then she'd only be a phone call away to talk Emma through the hard stuff. It figured that the one time Emma *really* needed her, Grandma Grace was off on a one-month honeymoon cruise around the world with her new husband, Elliot. What was he thinking in taking her grandma on some huge ship way out in the ocean and making her completely unreachable? She wasn't due back until more than a week after Emma had to turn in Allegra's collection to *Madison*.

Emma stood and walked around her worktable a few times. Shake it off, she told herself. You can do this. Just go slowly but confidently—that's what Grandma Grace would say. The minute the machine thinks it's controlling you and you're not controlling it, you're doomed. Be the boss!

Emma sat back down, picked up the garment pieces, and positioned them in the machine. She pressed her foot down on the pedal to start the motor. But within seconds, the sleeve was bunched up and crooked. She yanked everything out, removed the botched stitches, and tried again. And then again. After five tries, she still couldn't get it right.

She needed to get these sleeves done today so she could stay on schedule. She grabbed her cell off the table behind her. She hit the speed dial and held her breath. She didn't want to bother her grandmother on her honeymoon, but this was an emergency—and Emma was desperate. She knew her grandmother, who loved making clothes as much as Emma did, would totally understand why Emma needed to interrupt her cruise.

The call went right into voice mail. Emma jammed her finger down on the red button. Great. No service.

Emma debated calling Charlie. If it were a Paige issue, she wouldn't have hesitated. But what would

Charlie possibly do about a misaligned sleeve? She looked around her empty studio, the force of the realization hitting her like an oncoming city bus. I'm on my own, she thought. When it comes to making the clothes, I'm really on my own.

She couldn't decide if that was scary...or exciting. It might just be both.

"Do you have the invoices from August ready?" Marjorie asked.

"August...yes, I have them here," Emma said, flipping through the stack on her lap. Emma had made the mistake fifteen minutes earlier of pacing out of her studio to calm herself. Caught *not* working at work, she had no choice but to drop the sleeve problem and deal with the invoice problem. Normally, it wasn't a big deal—going through invoices with Marjorie—but today every minute away from her sleeve and her studio felt like hours.

Marjorie slowly read off the names of companies and the shipments they sent. Way too slowly.

"You can go faster," Emma suggested. "Or maybe we can switch, and I can read off the list."

Marjorie took off her glasses and raised a pre-arched, penciled eyebrow at Emma. "What's going on over there? You got somewhere better to be?"

"Not really," Emma said as she fidgeted in the uncomfortable vinyl guest chair. "I just have a lot going on right now." Like sleeves that won't align, Emma thought, and the English paper I haven't even started yet that's due tomorrow. And all the sewing I have to do in less than a week.

"Anything I can help with? A big project, maybe?" Marjorie asked.

Emma froze. Does Marjorie know something? There's no way *Marjorie* could've figured out the Allegra thing—is there? "I don't think so...but thanks."

"Okay, then." Marjorie put her glasses back on. "Let's see. Where was I? Do you have the one for Global Lace Mills?"

Just then, Emma's phone tucked in her jeans' pocket buzzed. She slid it out slightly, peeking at the screen. A text from Paige Young. What could Paige want? Marjorie was still reading through the list no faster than before. Emma squirmed in her seat.

"I think that covers August, unless you have any extra invoices there," Marjorie said, looking over the top of her rhinestone-embellished reading glasses. Emma wasn't quite sure if Marjorie wore them to be retro cool (which they were!), or if she just hadn't stopped wearing them since the first time they were in style.

"Nope—we're all set. I just need to go to the bathroom.

I'll be back in a second." Emma tossed her pile of papers on Marjorie's desk and dashed down the hall and into the warehouse. She pulled out her phone.

> Ms. B: Need sumthing 4 online preview of Designers 2 Watch section. Can I come by ur studio 2 see ur collection & take some digi-photos? Pls advise. Ciao, PY

Here? I can't have Paige come here, Emma thought. There's nothing to see, because I've barely started. She gripped the phone so tightly her knuckles turned red. How could she possibly put off Paige without making her suspicious? Emma speed-dialed Charlie.

"What's up?" Charlie said.

Emma told him about Paige's request as she walked quickly back and forth up the dark aisles lined with boxes and bolts of lace. "What do I do?"

Charlie was quiet for a minute. "Hmm. That's a tricky one. How about you tell Paige that Allegra has like, a policy that she doesn't allow editors to see her stuff while she's working on it?"

Emma paused as she let that idea sink in. "That sounds sort of believable, I guess. But wait—how will I explain why Paige was able to see Allegra's dresses when she first came to Laceland?"

"Easy," Charlie replied. "Paige wasn't *supposed* to see the dresses that time, remember? She just happened to be at Laceland and was being nosy and found the dresses herself. Not that you'd say it that way, but you know what I mean. She wasn't *invited* to see the dresses. So you could just say that Allegra's interns—meaning us—were new and didn't know her policy."

"You're right. Okay, that works. Got it. I have to get off so I can send the text and get back to Marjorie." Emma's eyes slid toward the hallway to make sure Marjorie wasn't looking for her.

"I'll let you go right after you admit that I am a brilliant mastermind," he said.

"Oh, please!" Emma laughed. "Fine. Good-bye, brilliant mastermind!"

Emma quickly typed a text to Paige explaining her "policy" and pressed send. She took a few steps back toward the reception area, and her phone vibrated again.

OK. Can I get them 1 or 2 days early so I can c them b4 my boss does? Need 2 know what I'm working with ahead of time. I can't afford any surprises.

Emma frantically typed her response.

Sorry but I need every minute until the deadline 2 get everything just right. Can't rush the process. Will b worth the wait, u'll c! AB

Emma squeezed her eyes shut and held her breath for sixty beats. Please let Paige be cool with that, Emma wished, clutching the phone between her hands as she counted...56, 57, 58...At 59, the phone began vibrating furiously, one angry buzz after the other, faster than she could read through the sudden avalanche of messages.

NOW I'm worried. U r going 2 b finished by Monday, rite? I'm counting on u! My job, no my CAREER, depends on u delivering on time & sending FABULOUS stuff!!!

My reputation is on the line. I fought like crazy 4 u 2 b included in the feature. If u don't deliver the spread will b empty & I will b FIRED!

My ed-in-chief is a perfectionist tyrant in couture. She wldnt blink 2x b4 firing an editor over failing 2 produce what she's promised. Seen it happen.

Plenty stiletto-wearing vultures circling here 2 take my job & plenty more designers who'd kill 2 take urs! This is OUR chance. Pls pls pls don't let me down!

Promise me u will b done on time. If not, I'll have 2 find a replacement, like yesterday. Not my preference AT ALL. But will do it if I have 2.

P.S. Thank u. Ciao, PY

Emma typed out what she hoped would be her last response for the day.

> U will get my designs on Monday, guaranteed. They will b completely finished & fabulous, guaranteed. U dont need 2 find a replacement. I AM ur Designer 2 Watch.

"Emma?" her dad called as he entered her work space an hour later. "Emma!" he shouted over the roar of the sewing machine.

Emma lifted her foot off the pedal. After she was finally done with Marjorie and the invoicing, she'd raced back to her studio. She'd flung the frustrating jacket sleeve on her work table and grabbed the pattern pieces for the vest. She needed to get at least one thing done by the end of the day, and she thought that she could sew together the outer fabric of the vest quickly. No such luck. She had designed it with four outside patch pockets with flaps that needed perfect seams since they'd be visible. Plus the flaps had to line up perfectly over the pockets. But so far she had only managed to finish one. She knew the construction of these pieces had to be flawless.

"What's up?" Emma asked, as pulled all the flyaway pieces of her hair back into the ponytail.

"Ready to go? I thought you were going to meet me up

front at six." He was wearing his jacket and carrying his nylon briefcase.

Oh, no! She hadn't realized the time. "But I'm not ready yet. I still have so much to do," Emma explained, the words from Paige's earlier texts still swirling around in her head. "Can't we stay a little longer? An hour? A half hour?"

"Nope. I'm beat. I got here really early today. And it's my night to cook," her dad explained.

"Can I please-please-please stay? I'll leave soon, I promise."

He frowned. "You know I'm not leaving you here alone after hours. The security guards go off duty after six."

"What about Isaac?" Emma suggested. "When's he leaving?"

"He's already gone. Had tickets to a food festival downtown. The other warehouse guys are gone, too," he said. "Come on, it's late." He turned to leave.

What now? Emma racked her brain for a solution. She needed more time. She only had a couple of days with her sewing machine before Saturday arrived. Who knows if I'll be able to get into Laceland over the weekend? She'd worry about that later. Right now, she had to figure out a way to stay and finish the vest.

"Is Marjorie still here? Can I at least ask her?" Emma begged.

Her dad snorted. "I love Marjorie Kornbluth, but I

don't think the woman has worked late a day in her life. But if you want to ask her, be my guest."

Emma raced by her father toward the reception area. Marjorie was reapplying her frosted pink lipstick—a sure sign she was about to leave. And considering how impatient Emma acted earlier, Marjorie probably wasn't about to trip over herself to do something for Emma.

"Marjorie! Can you please do me the hugest favor in the world? Could you stay like another hour while I work on something? Noah needs to leave and—"

"He won't let her stay here alone," he finished for his daughter, as he joined them up front. His eyes twinkled in a mischievous way, as they often did. He thought it was funny that Emma was asking Marjorie.

Marjorie looked back and forth between Emma and Noah as she tucked her mirrored, enamel compact and lipstick tube back in her purse. "I don't know about that. I have plans, and I—"

"Please?" Emma interlaced her hands together in front of her chest. "I promise to do all the billing for a week." *After* my collection is done, she added in her head.

Marjorie tilted her wrist to look at her delicate antique watch. "I *suppose* I could stay a little longer. I'm not meeting my sister for dinner downtown until about eight, and it doesn't make sense to go all the way uptown just to turn around an hour later. If this is all right with you, Noah. I'll lock up and put her in a cab when I leave."

Noah frowned slightly as he considered the plan. "You have cab money?" he asked Emma. She put out her hand and accepted the ten dollars he dropped into it, having spent every last penny on fabric. "Okay. Be home at seven-thirty, or your mom will kill us both."

"Thanks, Dad." She gave him a quick hug. "And thanks, Marjorie! I owe you one." Emma returned to her sewing machine, adrenaline pumping and raring to sew.

But the fairly ancient machine wasn't in the mood to cooperate with her need for speed-stitching. It fought back by pricking her finger with the needle over and over again. Her grandmother should've mentioned that the Singer had a temper! She wrapped her fingers in Band-Aids and pushed on. But the only thing that was moving forward was the time. It was now six-forty, but Emma wasn't any closer to finishing the pockets.

"Arrgh!" Emma cried out after another needle prick, this time through the Band-Aid. "Why won't you behave?"

"Who's not behaving?" Marjorie asked, suddenly appearing out of the shadows of the darkened warehouse and into the pool of light flooding Emma's work space.

"This...stupid...machine!" Emma blurted. "And these annoying vest pockets!"

"Hmm," Marjorie said, taking in the scene, "you certainly seem to have your hands full here, honey. This is no rinky-dink operation. What's all this for?"

Emma's back stiffened as she remembered Marjorie didn't know—couldn't know—the truth. If Marjorie knew, then her dad would know, and then her mom would know, and then, well, Emma wasn't sure how she'd react. And there was no way her dad would keep this kind of info from her mom. He was always saying they were a "team."

"It's, uh, an art project for school, and I really need an A. I didn't complete some other assignments, and the teacher said that if I didn't—"

Marjorie rolled her eyes and waved Emma off with her hand. "Spare me the soap opera. Who do you think has been dodging all those calls from Paige Young? Who didn't let her back here when she came by the other day demanding to see *Allegra Biscotti*? I know I wasn't born yesterday, but seriously, I wasn't born yesterday."

Emma gaped at Marjorie. Did she hear that correctly? Paige was looking for Allegra—*here?* Of course! It suddenly made total sense that Paige would come back to the place where she first saw Allegra's designs to find her. No wonder Paige was having a total text-message meltdown.

"Don't bother denying it," Marjorie continued. "I'm not mad or anything. While you were in school, I saw what you had going on back here. I put two and two together. I'm smart like that," she said, tapping her finger to her temple.

So Marjorie *did* figure it out!

After Noah had given Emma her work space, Marjorie had never once asked Emma what she was up to when she brought in shopping bags from Allure. Emma thought Marjorie hadn't even noticed—or cared. "Does…does my dad know?" Emma stammered.

"Nah." Marjorie shrugged. "I figured you had your reasons not to tell him. Besides, I make it a rule never to get involved in office politics…or family matters," she added with an arch of her eyebrow.

Emma felt her shoulders slide down a couple of inches away from her ears. "Oh, thank you!"

Marjorie reached for her reading glasses, which hung from her neck on a beaded chain, and placed them on the bridge of her nose. Then she picked up Emma's design sketch of the vest, as well as the close-up sketches of how the pockets were meant to go, wrinkling her nose as she studied them.

"Slide over," Marjorie commanded.

Still in shock over all the new information she just learned, Emma did as she was told, abandoning the chair in front of the sewing machine. Marjorie leaned over to inspect the two pockets Emma had sewn on.

"I think I see what's going on here..." Marjorie said. Then she fiddled with some settings, lowered the presser foot and then the needle, revved up the motor, and let it rip.

"What are you doing?" Emma cried in horror. "Wait! Stop! You'll ruin it!"

IT'S TECHNICAL

Don't worry!" Marjorie shouted over the hum of the sewing machine's motor and the rapid-fire clack-clack-clack of the needle going up and down and in and out of the fabric. "I'm a professional. In my old life, I used to be a seamstress in the alterations department at Bergdorf Goodman."

"Are you kidding me?" Emma stared in amazement as Marjorie whizzed over the seam, expertly going around the edge of the pocket piece at what seemed to Emma like hair-raising speed. "Why haven't you ever told me?"

"Because you never asked," Marjorie replied. "I did have a life before Laceland, you know."

When Marjorie finished, she let up on the foot pedal, raised the needle and the presser foot, and pulled the vest out to the left. Then she took Emma's scissors and snipped the two threads.

"Let's see what we have here," Marjorie said, examining her own seam, as well as Emma's work on the rest of the piece. "Not bad here, honey. Nice even seams. Pockets can be tricky, so don't beat yourself up."

Emma leaped forward and grabbed the vest from Marjorie's hands. "This is amazing! Thank you, thank you, thank you!"

"Sure thing. If you'd like, I can sew the other one so you can see how I'm doing it…without mutilating my fingers in the process." She nodded down at Emma's Band-Aid covered hands. "I can even help you with those jacket sleeves."

Marjorie my ANGEL

"How did you know I was having trouble with those?" Emma asked.

Marjorie pointed with a bony finger at the worktable where the body of the jacket and the still unconnected sleeves sat in a heap.

"They're the worst if you're not used to them. Used to trip me up all the time, too. Besides, from the looks of it, I'd say there isn't much room on your fingers for more Band-Aids."

Emma wanted to hug Marjorie. But Marjorie didn't strike her as the embracing type. Instead Emma handed her the pieces of the fourth vest pocket.

"I think I'm going to be a vampire," Kayla announced the next day by Holly's locker. "My mom said she could have one of the makeup artists from her company do my face for the party—you know, white skin, charcoal around the eyes, long fake lashes, and blood-red lips. How cool would that be?"

"What are you going to wear?" Lexie asked.

"Who cares?" Kayla replied. "My makeup will be killer—literally!" she giggled. "Ivana, did you decide on your costume yet?"

"A Hollywood starlet," Ivana said smugly. "Very retro, you know...early sixties Marilyn Monroe glamour. I'm borrowing my mother's low-cut black gown, and I bought some superlong white leather gloves. I've already booked a blowout."

Emma tried not to eavesdrop, but that was technically impossible with her locker next to Holly's and the 'Bees overflowing into what little space she had. She was shocked to realize that Halloween was this Saturday. She'd been so

focused on her deadline. And she was kind of surprised that she hadn't heard about Kayla's Halloween party.

True, she had been ditching lunch in the cafeteria to spend it in the library in a desperate attempt to keep up with her homework, but she realized she must have totally tuned out life at Downtown Day to miss something so obviously huge on the school's social barometer.

"What about you, Holls?" Ivana asked.

"I don't know yet. Maybe an angel or a devil or something like that. I was going to go shopping after school at the costume store near my apartment, if anyone wants to come."

Lexie and Shannon said they'd join since they were still undecided. The bell rang, sending Ivana and her entourage sauntering to class. Holly hung back.

"You're coming to the party, right?"

"Maybe." Emma gathered her things, closed her locker, and headed down the almost empty hall. Holly was two steps behind her.

"Emma, you should totally come to the party," Holly urged. "I bet with all the cool things in your closet you could put together an outrageous costume."

"I didn't think I was invited. Besides, it doesn't seem like Ivana and the 'Bees want me there."

"Of course, you're invited! *Everyone's* invited!" Holly protested.

Emma stopped and turned to face Holly. "Really? I know I've been busy and all, but I don't remember getting an invitation—or even hearing anything about it before a few minutes ago."

The encouraging smile faded from Holly's face. "Well, um, *technically?* You weren't invited like *separately* or anything because everyone assumed you'd be coming. None of us got invitations either. Plus I can bring whoever I want because I'm practically co-hosting the party. And according to me, you're invited. Technically."

Emma was confused. But she had a feeling that was exactly the reaction Holly was going for as a way to cover up the *technical* lack of invitation. "Well then, thanks, I guess."

The smile instantly returned to Holly's face. "So does that mean you'll come? You wouldn't want to miss another chance to hang out with Jackson now that you guys have actually spoken, would you?"

At the sound of his name, Emma remembered the feel of his shirt against her cheek during the assembly the week before. Holly didn't even know that Jackson had walked by Emma's locker the other day and actually said hi to her—in front of a couple of his soccer buddies.

"I'll try," Emma hedged, knowing that she would need

a miracle—beyond the already huge one of discovering Marjorie could sew and was teaching her how to deal with the more complicated seams—to give her enough extra time to figure out a costume *and* be able to spend a whole night at a party, away from her sewing.

Holly's eyebrows knitted together. "That's it? You'll '*try*'? I just don't get it, Em. You know, I've really put myself out there with Ivana, telling her how cool and awesome you are, but you do nothing to show her any of that. You don't even *try*. You act like you're all superior or something. It puts people off, Emma."

Emma stiffened. Was she really acting that way? Or was Holly bending the truth? I'm acting like I'm superior to *Ivana?* Oh, please. How was that even possible? Who's the one with the fan page for herself? Emma was dying to ask. Not me!

"Look," Emma started, trying not to let her voice shake, "if you want to hang out with Ivana and all of them, just go ahead and do it. I didn't mean to get in your way."

"But I want to hang out with *you*, too," Holly said. "Don't you want to spend time with me?" She shifted on her feet. Her expression hardened ever so slightly but just enough for Emma to notice. "Look, if our friendship means something, you'll come to the party. Besides, Em, it's going to be *fun*. Remember fun?"

Feeling guilty, although for what she wasn't exactly sure, Emma relented. "Okay, okay. I'll go. For you."

"Good," Holly said, her face softening again.

"Happy now?"

"Yes. I am." And for the first time in weeks, Emma could see the old Holly—the real Holly—in her eyes.

For the rest of the day, Emma found it impossible to concentrate in her classes. Her body was so tired from staying up late, hand-sewing the detailed trimmings, that she felt almost weightless. Her foot tap-tap-tapped under the desk, anxious to press the pedal on the sewing machine and get back to work.

Emma opened to a fresh page in her sketchbook, as the rest of her world history classmates chatted before Ms. Lyons arrived, and made a list of the things she still needed to do before Monday. Delivery Day.

Construct dress and sew in zipper
Sew jacket lining (collar, cuffs, box pleat)
Attach vest lining with interior slit pockets
Sew dress lining (slit, belt)
Add buttons to vest and jacket

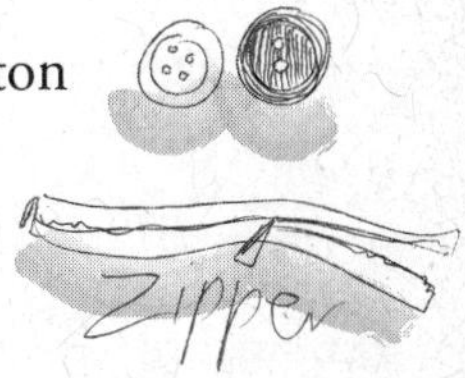

"Wearing costumes isn't my thing," Clayton Vanderbeck said, and Emma tuned back in. "Maybe I'll go to Kayla's party dressed as me."

Zipper

"That would be a scary disguise," teased Meghan Mahon, who definitely had a thing for Clayton. She giggled. "Or you could be a soccer player."

"Yeah, that would totally work since you're already pretending to be one on the field!" one of the other guys said. Everyone laughed, and the guy began ribbing Clayton about how he messed up a game the day before. Emma tuned back out. She sketched the vest button placement on the corner of the homework sheet she'd actually managed to complete the previous night.

"Hey, you going?"

Jackson Creedon. He was looking right at Emma with those eyes. Those amazing blue eyes. And talking to her.

"Oh, yeah, *totally*," she said.

"Cool."

"Are you?" she ventured, not wanting their second conversation to end—ever.

"Yeah."

"Class!" Ms. Lyons called out as she entered the room. "Let's get started."

Emma felt as if she were really filled with helium, hovering high above the classroom. Not only did Jackson *specifically* ask if she was going to Kayla's party, but also, and maybe more importantly, he thought it was "cool" that she was!

She couldn't wait to tell him about how she'd read—well,

looked at—*Night below the Surface.* We'll have so much more to talk about than the last time, Emma thought happily. She pictured them standing on the terrace at Kayla's apartment, maybe a moon rising over the city as the party went on inside. She'd be wearing that adorable fringed flapper dress she'd picked up at the vintage store last year—and that had been living in the back of her closet—and maybe fishnet stockings and her high-heeled, velvet peep-toe pumps.

First they'd talk about *Night below the Surface*, and then he'd ask a zillion great questions about her collection. He'd listen to her answers really hard, maybe biting his lip as he told her how much more interesting she was than any other girl in school. He would have such a hard time ending their fascinating conversation that he would offer to take her home…

She looked down at her list. In between "Sew jacket lining" and "Attach vest lining," she added, "Accessorize flapper costume for Kayla's party."

Emma clicked her phone shut. Charlie had called—again. Checking on her progress. She knew he felt frustrated. He wanted to do something, but really what was there for him to do? Only she could design and make the clothes.

She had just finished another successful afternoon sewing marathon at Laceland, thanks to Marjorie. Everything was slowly coming together. A full day of sewing tomorrow, Saturday, and she'd be close to done. Marjorie had agreed to meet her there to unlock the door, keep her company, and as they both knew, jump in and save Emma when she hit a snag.

While Emma waited for the elevator in the lobby of her apartment building, she thought about the pieces tucked in her bag that needed hand-sewing and that she would work on later tonight. She hoped she'd brought the right color thread. Her dad had taken the subway home with her but detoured at the corner to pick up the dry cleaning. As she fumbled around in her bag for her keys, which she could never find, her phone rang. No doubt it was Charlie. Again.

Resting the phone on her shoulder, she continued hunting. "Charlie, get a life!"

"Um...excuse me? Emily?" a perky female voice asked. Definitely not Charlie.

"Not Emily. Emma," Emma said, stepping onto the

elevator, hand still searching through the random buttons, pencils, and papers scattered in her bag.

"Oh. Sorry. I wanted Emily."

Emma finally felt her fingers graze the charm on her key ring. It was a thimble from an old Monopoly game. As a kid, she always picked the thimble. "I think you have the wrong number."

Emma stuffed her cell back into her bag, unlocked both locks on her front door, and walked into her apartment. She was hoping that her mom was out somewhere with William. Maybe today was his day with his tutor or when his computer-graphics club met. She could use a few minutes to decompress.

No such luck. Her mother walked out from the kitchen, wiping her hands on a dish towel. Her mouth was set in a hard grimace. Never a good sign.

"Hey, Mom." Emma hung her brown trench over a pile of off-season coats layered on the coatrack. "I'm starving. What's for dinner?"

Her mother's frown deepened. "We need to talk. I need to know what's been going on with you."

"What do you mean?" Emma's stomach tightened.

"Come on, Em. I think you know exactly what I'm talking about." Her mother paused, waiting for her daughter to fill in the blank.

Was the blank Allegra Biscotti? Emma fumbled for a response. Was she walking into a trap?

Her mother crossed her arms and continued. "Your grades, Emma? I checked them online today. You got a D on your geometry quiz. And a C-minus on your biology test. And there was a note about you turning in your essay on *War of the Worlds* three days late."

"I had a hard time keeping the SSS postulate and the ASA postulate straight," Emma explained. That wasn't even a lie. She really was confused by the whole proving congruent triangles thing—mostly because she hadn't been doing the homework. But she kept that part to herself.

Emma's father pushed open the front door and stopped. The mother-daughter tension hit him like a force field. He looked back and forth between them. "What'd I miss?"

As her mother filled him in, his smile faded. "Emma. This isn't good."

She shifted from foot to foot, staring at the worn wooden floor. Her parents had her cornered in the hallway. There was nowhere to go. "Geometry and biology have gotten really hard, and I—"

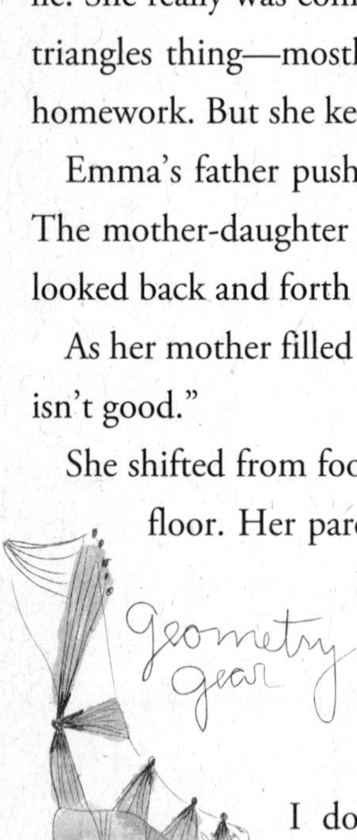

Her mother cut her off. "Please. I don't think this has anything to do with the material being over your head, especially this early in the year. It's obvious you're not studying. It's always been a simple equation. When you study, you do well."

Her mother sighed, as if pained. "From what your dad tells me, it isn't because he's been working you too hard at the warehouse, even though you've been spending every free second there lately."

"I've been…I'm working on some designs in my studio that I'm really into and…" Emma searched for a possible excuse.

William wandered in, his eyes glued to his portable video-game player. No doubt he'd heard the sounds of a serious conversation and came to investigate. And to make sure they weren't talking about him.

"I thought you were studying back there, at least part of the time," her father said. "That's why I tried not to give you too much other work to do."

"I am, I was…I mean, I'm also…" Emma stopped. Maybe it was time to tell the truth. It wasn't so bad, really. It was actually quite good. *I'm designing clothes for a fashion magazine*, she thought. *It's not like I'm some messed-up kid.*

"You're also what?" her mother asked with a mix of frustration and annoyance. Not a good combination. "What are you doing that you think is so much more important than your schoolwork? This I'd love to hear."

"She's been sewing!" William announced triumphantly.

"Sewing? Emma, are you kidding me? You know school comes first."

"I do. I'm studying—"

"Oh, yeah, right. I bet you've been staying up super-late every night because you've been *studying* so much," William piped in.

"Get out, William!" Emma snapped. "It's none of your business."

"Don't yell at your brother," her mother warned, all her negative energy fixed on Emma.

"Me? He's the one who butted in—" Emma couldn't believe how unfair her mother was being.

Her father shushed William and shook his head, shooting him that meaningful parent stare that said, Stay out of this one.

"Okay, let's just calm down here for a minute," he said in an even voice. Her dad was always the calm one. "It's obvious to me that something's got to give. You need to boost your grades. Okay, that shouldn't be a big issue for you. But until you do that, no more hanging out at Laceland—"

"No way!" Emma shot back, outrage shaping her words. "You can't do that!" Not now. He couldn't be saying that now.

"You're treading on thin ice with that attitude," her mother warned, her voice steely.

"I don't have an attitude," Emma retorted. Her body trembled, the blood rushing to her head. Why couldn't her mother just back down and listen? She hadn't even gotten to tell them yet. "You just don't understand. I need to work on these clothes I'm making—"

"Enough. It's enough, Emma. No sewing until the grades improve. End of story." Her mother turned back toward the kitchen.

Emma forced herself to take a deep breath and start over before she really blew it. "I'll fix it. I promise I'll bring my grades up."

"And the Western civ exam?" her mother asked.

"That, too. I have a full week before the test, right? I'll be ready."

"Good, you'll start tomorrow. All day at home studying. I can even help you."

"But…but I have plans tomorrow." Emma wished she didn't sound as if she were whining. But she was. She had to spend Saturday at Laceland.

"Cancel them." Her mother wasn't going to budge—that was obvious.

"Dad?" Emma gulped, looking helplessly at him.

"Sorry, Em. You're home studying—all day. Your mom and I, we're a team, you know."

"So I've heard," Emma grumbled. She stomped to her bedroom, but not before shooting William an icy stare.

I am not giving up, she promised herself, as she lay on her

bed. Tears formed in the corners of her eyes, but she pushed them away with the back of her hand and squeezed her lids tightly shut.

Coco would not cry, she knew.

Neither would Allegra Biscotti.

Coco would push on, defying despair and disbelievers in order to create that famous little black dress.

Allegra Biscotti, too, would do whatever it took to finish the pieces.

And so will I, she decided.

LIVING IN THE NOW

On Saturday morning, Emma awoke, still determined but without a plan.

She had called Charlie right after the big fight, and he was thinking of a way out. Literally. But so far he had nothing good. His newest plan had him meeting Marjorie at Laceland and smuggling her heavy sewing machine and the partially finished clothes to the apartment. It wasn't the most devious or ingenious idea, but all Emma knew was, no matter what, she had to get to her sewing machine.

She walked into the kitchen, deciding to ignore what happened last night. Today, she'd be the sweet, studious daughter. It was easier that way.

"Morning, Mom." Emma broke off a piece of one of the blueberry muffins on the table. Her mom was actually a good baker. Emma wondered if baking wasn't a schoolteacher thing for her mom, too, with following a recipe maybe just like reading another novel. Except with baking, Emma decided, the story ended much better—with cookies or muffins.

Her mother took a sip of her giant mug of coffee, the weekend section of the newspaper unfolded in front of her. "You're up early for a Saturday. Going to hit the books?"

Emma knew that wasn't a question. "Yeah," she responded, filling a glass with orange juice. "Where's Dad?"

"He had to take William to his tutoring session across town. Then I'm going to meet up with them to do some errands. You'll have the whole apartment to yourself for studying. No interruptions. Or distractions." She eyed Emma over the top of her glasses.

"Okay, great." Emma grabbed the rest of the muffin. She began to calculate the possibilities. If her parents were going to be out all day, she could go to Laceland. They wouldn't even have to know she was gone. Emma hesitated. On the sneaky scale, this was pretty high. But she also couldn't risk losing a whole day of sewing—especially when she was so close to finishing.

Back in her room, she called Charlie. He liked the plan, of course. She felt guilty. Of course.

"If I get caught, I can't even imagine the enormous trouble I'll be in," she told Charlie.

"Em, you've done too much. You're too far in. There's no choice, really. You have to finish. So you have to sneak out."

Charlie always made everything sound so connect-the-dots easy.

"There'll be consequences," she warned.

"Look, you worry too much about what's *going* to happen. You need to live in *now*."

"True," Emma reasoned. "And my collection will be done on Monday. Then everything will go back to normal."

"And your parents will never know," Charlie concluded.

"Charlie." Emma paused, trying desperately not to get swept up in the wave of self-doubt that was trying so hard to flood her brain this week. "What if Paige hates my new stuff? What then?"

"Then no more Allegra Biscotti. You make honor roll and take that Western civ class. And you still live happily ever after."

"I'd be happier if she liked them."

"Then get out of that apartment."

Two hours later, she met Marjorie and Charlie at Laceland.

"What's in the mystery case?" Emma asked. Marjorie stood in the middle of Emma's studio in what must be her weekend outfit—black knit pants and a black ribbed turtleneck—with a large black rectangular case by her side.

"My sewing machine."

Emma's eyes widened. Of all the people in her life to become her fashion angel, Emma never would have picked Marjorie. "Oh, wow, Marjorie. That's the most amazing thing. You didn't have to, you know."

"I know, believe me. But I'm here anyway, so I might as well really help. I didn't travel fifty blocks downtown just to open a door. Let's get to work."

Side by side, they sewed silently back in Emma's studio. Emma constructed each piece, meticulously double-checking each nearly invisible intersecting seam. After every seam or dart was added, she carefully tried the garment on the dress form, making minute alterations for a perfect fit.

She wished she had a fit model—a living, moving person—instead of a fabric dress-form replica, but her own body was far from the willowy model type. And Marjorie's was even farther. There were no other options, so she'd just have to cross her fingers that the garments would drape and move properly when worn by a real person.

Marjorie worked the iron, carefully pressing each section of fabric so it wouldn't wrinkle or pucker. She also handled the finishing work—adjusting hemlines, removing the basting seams, and then adding the permanent ones.

Charlie was in charge of tunes and food. He was on a run now to a nearby deli for sandwiches, drinks, and real coffee for Marjorie.

"What's next?" Marjorie asked Emma.

"I've finished most of the dress, but I'm having some trouble getting the slit right without pulling this fabric. It's so delicate...but I had to have it."

"Here, hand it over." Marjorie reached for the pinned pieces of fabric. She spent a few minutes reviewing Emma's detailed sketches and patterns before gently placing the pieces in her own sewing machine.

Emma glanced around her studio. There was still a lot left to do—attaching closures, adding cuffs, making the belt, and of course, sewing in the finished linings on all three pieces—and she felt odd, just watching Marjorie perfect the slit for her.

"This isn't cheating, is it? By having you help me sew?" Emma asked.

Marjorie took her foot off the pedal, and the whirring motor slowing stopped. "Of course not, honey. I'm just the worker bee here. You don't think Ralph Lauren does all his own sewing, do you?"

Suddenly, they heard the creaking of floorboards.

Marjorie raised her eyebrows at Emma. Emma shrugged, unsure of the noise.

Then they heard the footsteps. The unmistakable rhythm

of footsteps approaching the back of the warehouse. Approaching *them*.

Emma's eyes grew wide. "It doesn't sound like Charlie," she whispered. That was, not unless he brought the deli staff back with him. There was definitely more than one person.

The footsteps moved forward, the sound of shoes hitting the floorboards echoing off the high ceilings.

Marjorie grabbed the fabric shears, gripping them tightly in her delicate hands.

Emma peered toward the darkened hall, but she couldn't see anything in the dim light. Her breath caught in her throat. She reached into her bag, quickly wrapping her fingers around her cell phone.

Flipping it open, she began to dial. 9…the keypad tone rang out loudly in the eerie silence, causing her to cringe. 1… the footsteps stopped.

"Who's there?" a deep voice called.

Emma stopped dialing. She knew that voice.

In the light of the opening to Emma's work space, her father appeared. Her mother and William stood behind him.

"Emma!" her father cried, alarmed. Then his eyes darted to Marjorie, gripping the scissors like a dagger. "Marjorie?"

"What…what're you guys doing here?" Emma blurted out, a jumble of relief and panic.

"What are *you* doing here?" her mother demanded, the

furrow lines in her forehead deepening with every word. "You're supposed to be at home studying."

"I didn't think you'd be here," Emma said lamely. She was too overwhelmed to create even more lies.

"That's obvious," her dad said in a measured tone. Emma could see he was just as angry as her mom. It didn't happen often but when it did…it wasn't good. "I had something to do here. In *my* office. But I think right now you're the one with explaining to do."

Marjorie stood up to leave. "I think I'll just go, uh, do something else."

Emma saw a look pass between Marjorie and Noah as she slid by the Roses on her way out of the work space. She had no idea what that look meant, but she was too nervous to worry about that right now.

"What's going on here?" her dad demanded. "This isn't like you, sneaking around behind our backs like this."

Her dad, her mom, and even William stared at her, waiting. For once, William wasn't smirking. He actually looked kind of scared.

There was no way she couldn't tell them now. She knew that. She took a deep breath and began to explain—everything.

"Dad, do you remember Paige Young?" she began.

As Emma continued, Noah and Joan exchanged many concerned glances, but to Emma's surprise, sometimes they smiled ever so slightly when she described the high points—Paige putting Allegra in her blog, *Madison* picking up the post, the interview on the *Madison* website, and then, of course, the request for Allegra's pieces to be photographed for the actual pages of the most influential magazine in the fashion industry.

When she finished, Emma felt like she had just run a hundred miles. Or spent the last two weeks working night and day on three brand-new garments while attending high school.

Her dad leaned forward and pressed his palms flat against her worktable. "Why didn't you tell us? That's what I don't understand."

Emma looked up at the ceiling. She hated that the twinkle was gone from her father's eyes. What was worse was that Emma knew that she was responsible for that.

"The whole thing just seemed to happen so fast," she explained. "I'd do one thing and think that was it. But then Paige would ask for something else, and then something else...and the lie kept getting bigger and bigger somehow. I didn't know how to stop without ruining *everything*."

Her mother cleared her throat. That wasn't a good sign, Emma knew, so she braced herself.

"You know that I don't deal with lying, whatsoever, under any circumstance," her mother began, "especially lying to your parents."

"I agree. The lying thing is a really big deal," her dad said, looking directly into Emma's eyes. "I can maybe see how this spun out of control, but lying is not cool with us—at all. We need to be able to trust you."

"I get it," Emma said. And the funny thing was that she really *did.* "I'm *so* sorry. I really am. You can trust me."

"I hope so." Her mother paused, debating what to say next.

Emma couldn't chance it. She knew a punishment was heading her way—that was Prada-black-dress obvious. She had to step up, to show them that Allegra Biscotti was more than some random name she'd made up. That Allegra was a designer with talent. That Allegra was *her*. "Can I show you what I'm making?"

"I would hope so," her mom said. "Especially after all the effort you've made *not* to show us."

"Can I see, too?" William asked.

Emma had almost forgotten Will was there. He had been so quiet the whole time. "Definitely. Come over here."

Emma explained the inspiration, pointing to the pages from *Night below the Surface* and then the sketches she created for her own designs. She held up the lining fabrics, so her mother could see how they would eventually work with the dress, the jacket, and the vest. She showed them the garments in progress displayed on the three dress forms.

"Emma! They're stunning," Her mother gave her arm an enthusiastic squeeze. "They're like pieces of art! I honestly can't get over what you've accomplished in such a short time. I'm amazed! Truly."

Emma suddenly felt uncomfortable, unsure how to react to her mother's warm praise. She wasn't used to getting it on anything other than her grades. And even then, it wasn't especially the gushing kind because Emma was just doing what her mother already expected of her.

"I had some help," she said.

Her mother shook her head strongly. "Don't give away the credit. Emma, these were *your* visions. And not only did you dream up these amazing things, you brought them to life. *You* are the source. Creative vision is a rare and wonderful thing."

Emma was relieved that her mother was finally seeing what she had been trying to explain to her for so long.

"Now I'm a little stuck with what we should do about this whole situation." Her mom and dad exchanged looks, as if speaking a secret silent language. Then they walked outside the filing-cabinet walls and into the hallway for a private discussion. Emma couldn't guess what the verdict would be.

"Um...hi?" Charlie tentatively entered the studio with a large brown bag of turkey sandwiches in his hand. A glance at her conferring parents, Emma's stricken face, and the fact that Marjorie had taken off told him all he needed to know. "I hate it when I miss the previews," he whispered. "And something tells me the movie already started."

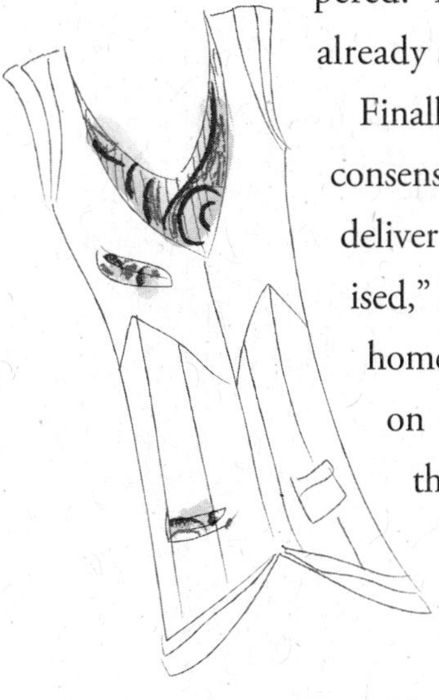

Finally Emma's parents returned, a consensus reached. "We'll let you finish and deliver to Paige Young what you promised," her dad said, "provided you do your homework tomorrow and go to school on Monday. But then on Tuesday, things have to go back to normal. No more sneaking around, going behind our backs, and ditching your schoolwork. And no lying."

"Totally," Emma said.

"And as punishment, no nights out with friends for the next month. School and then working for me in the afternoon and then home for homework—and that's it."

Emma didn't care if she never left her house again for the next year, if it meant she could finish her pieces.

"Thank you, thank you, thank you!" She leaped toward her parents, grabbing them both in a hug. "Now I just hope

I *make* the deadline. Even with Marjorie's help, I don't know if I can get everything done by Monday."

"You'll get it done, Cookie. No one knows their way around a sewing machine like Marjorie. And no one is a better designer than you, or should I say, Allegra." Her dad's eye twinkle was back.

"Why don't I go out to the front and get Marjorie?" her mother said. "Seems like you two have a long day ahead of you."

Her dad returned to Laceland at six o'clock that night. "Hey, Cookie. I saw Marjorie in the lobby. She looked wiped out. She said Charlie took off, too."

"Yeah, he needed to get home," Emma mumbled through several straight pins sticking out of the corner of her mouth. "We got through a lot, but I still have more to do. Thanks for coming back."

"No problem. Your mom and I didn't have any big plans for tonight. And I have some things I need to organize around here for tomorrow anyway. I'll order up some pizza for us."

Three hours and two large slices of veggie pizza later, Emma finally had constructed all the linings. She felt as if she'd hiked to the summit of a mountain. She needed to stretch her leg, which she worried might permanently vibrate from so many hours pressed to the sewing-machine pedal.

As she walked through the warehouse, she heard her dad grunting and groaning. Then something slammed to the floor.

She raced around the corner. "Dad? Are you all right?"

"I'm fine," he answered, rubbing his lower back. "Just moving some of these boxes. Or trying to."

"Do you need help?" she asked.

"Nah, I got it. You keep working on your stuff. I'll let you know when I'm ready to go."

"Okay." She took the long way back to her work space, making the most of her stretch break. Back at her sewing machine, just as she was about to press down on the pedal again, she heard a buzz and looked up. It was her phone, buried deep inside her bag on the worktable.

She pulled it out. Two missed calls and four text messages—all from Holly. That's strange, Emma thought. I guess I didn't hear the phone with the machine running.

Wanted 2 make sure u have Kayla's address. I'll b there early so come whenevs! Can't wait 2 c ur costume! U wont believe mine! xoH

R u coming? Everyone's here already & totally in costume, including JC, but dont want 2 ruin the surprise. Come soon! xoH

Em! Why rn't u picking up ur cell? Where r u?

Fine. Don't come. C if I care.

Emma sunk her head into her hands. She had forgotten all about Kayla's Halloween party…and Jackson!

She looked down at the clock on her phone. 9:17 p.m. *There's still time,* Emma thought, whipping around in her chair. *I can still figure out a costume and get over to Kayla's.* She began to stand and then stopped.

She wasn't going to any party tonight. She was grounded. And she certainly wasn't crazy enough to prance over to her dad and ask him to change his mind.

She fingered the long strip of sequined material she'd cut out for the belt. She turned it back and forth, amazed by the patterns of light that played off its shimmery surface. At every angle, the color changed.

She didn't feel like leaving right now anyway, she realized. Even though the possibility of getting together with Jackson made her lungs forget how to take in air. What she wanted to do, most of all, was sew. She was so close to seeing the dreams from her sketch pad become real. There was no putting the brakes on now. Especially not for a Halloween party.

Holls: So sorry! U wldnt believe what happened 2day—

Emma groaned and deleted the message. This wasn't the kind of thing you texted. It made her sound like she didn't care. After everything that had happened between them,

Holly would think her not showing meant she didn't want to be friends.

She needed to talk to Holly face-to-face. She tucked her phone away. It would be better to beg Holly for forgiveness tomorrow. As for Jackson, well, she could only pray to the God of Coco that this hadn't been her one and only chance.

But Sunday morning Holly wouldn't answer her cell or respond to Emma's emails. Emma kept count. Three calls directly to voice mail, four unanswered texts, and two emails sent into the netherworld. Holly obviously wanted nothing to do with her.

Emma had gotten up early that morning to tackle the mountain of homework. Her mother kept walking into the living room with the excuse of needing this book off the shelf or that folder from the desk, so Emma had no choice but to plow through. By lunchtime, she was almost caught up—or at least closer than she had been in two weeks. She tried Holly again. Silence. Total freeze-out.

Then, after lunch, disaster struck.

Emma and her father rode up to Laceland in the empty elevator. The ancient building was eerily silent on a Sunday. Emma's fingers itched to feel the hum of the machine under them again. She was so close now. Almost done. She practically sprinted to the front door, hopping from one foot to the other as she waited for her father to unlock it.

"It's open," he said. "Leo—you know, the building maintenance guy—is here with his team to do some repair work. But they shouldn't be in your way at all."

Emma pushed through the door and raced straight back to her work space. She froze, blinking several times. And screamed.

FLIPPED OUT!

She couldn't believe her eyes. Paint!

White paint...splattered everywhere.

A dirty canvas tarp was draped haphazardly on her worktable. The floor of her studio was littered with cans of open paint, metal trays, and wood mixing sticks. And on her dress forms...oh, God...she couldn't bear to look.

"No! No! Please no!" Emma screamed. "Dad! Come quick!"

Her father burst in. "What's wrong?"

She pointed with a shaking hand at one of the dress forms. Her vest. Her beautiful, smooth cotton-sateen gray vest with the silk aquatic-watercolor-design lining had two huge white paint splatters. "They *ruined* it!" Tears sprung to her eyes.

"I don't understand it." Her father stared, horrified. "They weren't supposed to be back here at all!" He balled his fists, his anger apparent. "Where is Leo? Leo! I paid him to supervise the painters just so something like this *wouldn't* happen. Leo!" He took a deep breath. "Are the other two pieces all right?"

Emma slowly walked over to the other two dress forms. She had left all three of her girls, as she had taken to calling them, here last night dressed in her nearly finished creations and looking beautiful. She had said a special good night to each one almost the same way her dad used to do when he tucked her in when she was younger. Wishing each one dreams as sweet as cotton candy. And now…now…

She examined the fabric as if under a microscope. She nodded slowly. The other two were unharmed. The third, oh God. She scrunched her eyes closed.

"I'm so, so sorry, Cookie," Noah said, shaking his head. "This is awful. Leo has never let me down before."

"What am I going to do?" Emma choked, as she tried to pick a glob of paint off the outside of the vest with her fingernail. But the paint was already dry. Even if she could scrape off the top layer, the fabric had already absorbed most of it.

"Is there any way you could send two pieces instead?"

"I can't. I promised—Allegra promised, whoever promised—Paige *three* pieces. Three, not two!" Emma gulped. "And if I don't deliver all three on time, she's going to find a designer to replace me. I'll be ruined before I ever get started."

Emma sunk to the floor, her legs too shaky to support her.

Now what?

Sunday passed in a blur. Charlie was summoned, of course. Her father screamed at Leo and his painters. Leo apologized profusely. But, really, what good did that do? The damage was done.

Charlie analyzed the situation from every angle. There was no question that two was not three, and three was what Paige wanted. Charlie advocated the quality-versus-quantity argument for a while. But Emma was no fool. Paige wanted it all—three new pieces, all to-die-for amazing. And Allegra had to deliver.

"So what about you just make another vest, identical to this one?" Charlie suggested. "Shouldn't it be easier the second time around?"

"If it were that simple, don't you think I would be working on it already?" Emma shot back. "It's Sunday. Allure is closed, and I don't have enough of the outer fabric or the lining fabric left over to start again. And even if I raced to Allure right after school tomorrow and bought more fabric, there's no way I'd be able to finish it in a couple of hours."

"Okay, skip school. Problem solved." Charlie crossed his arms, satisfied with his solution.

"Problem not solved. I promised my parents I was going to school tomorrow. I have to go." Emma ran her fingers nervously through her hair. She couldn't battle her mother now about missing school, on top of everything else. "Next idea?"

After a bout of tears and four big Reese's peanut-butter cups, Emma finally decided she would turn in her two new pieces along with the off-white linen corset dress she had made the previous summer. The dress didn't fit into her collection, but it was done, which, at this point, was a huge plus. Emma analyzed the dress. If she could include some of the lining material—Charlie crawled on the floor, gathering the useable scraps left over from the vest—and weave strips of it into the corset and maybe have some peeking out ever so slightly from the hem of the dress, the dress might not look like an afterthought. She hoped.

Emma felt as if she were in an action movie. Instead of running for her life, she was sewing at manic speed. She stitched as fast as she could without sacrificing the level of construction. She polished the other dress and the jacket until she felt they were perfect.

Then she tackled the corset dress, incorporating the lining fabric in what she hoped was an innovative design. During the entire afternoon, she could barely look at her ruined vest, still displayed on the dress form. Except for the finishing touches—and maybe a little extra work on the corset dress—Emma finished by Sunday night.

She truly loved the charcoal jacket and the belted dress.

She just wished she was happier with her last-minute corset dress. It was good, but she suspected it wasn't quite good enough. She could envision Paige shaking her head in disbelief, throwing around phrases such as, "overworked," "tacky," and "lacking vision." How humiliating! If she was going to fail at this, she decided, she couldn't fail with a dress she didn't believe in.

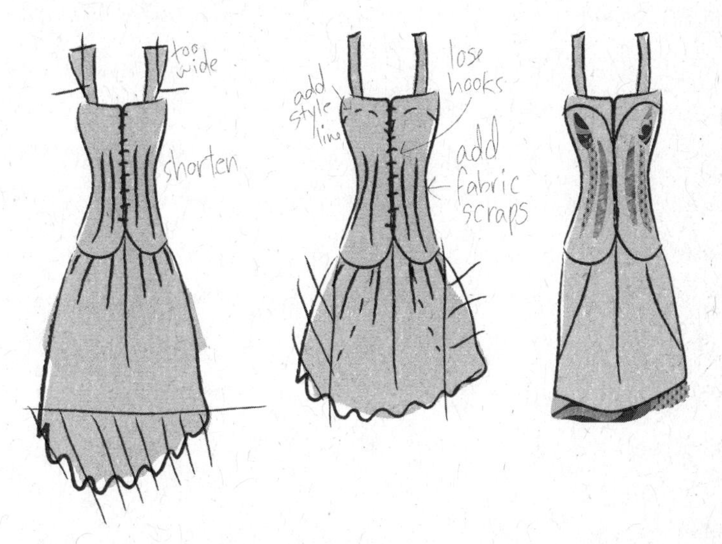

All night, Emma tossed and turned in bed, redesigning the dress in her mind. Adding fabric, taking away fabric. Changing the hemline. Altering the shape. As the variations appeared and morphed on the inside of her eyelids, she felt as if morning would never come, and then suddenly it was here.

She rode the subway to school next to her mother as usual, except this morning she played a different game in her sketchbook. This game was called: Reimagine the Dress.

Emma waited for Holly at her locker. She realized that Sunday had passed without them talking. She needed to make things right. But Holly didn't show. Emma shuffled into her first-period classroom and took her seat, her mind still focused on the dress. She now wondered if she shouldn't reroute to Allure after school and buy more fabric to try to line the skirt. Or was that just ridiculous?

"I've never seen Lexie that mad before!" Emma overheard Kayla say two rows in front of her.

"I know," Shannon agreed. She had the desk next to Kayla.

"You think she's going to stay mad at Holly forever? If I were Lexie, I would. I mean, Holly stole Lexie's boyfriend," Kayla said.

Emma leaned forward slightly in her desk chair to hear more.

"Seriously!" Shannon gasped. "Holly was totally hanging all over Jackson. By the end of the night, she was practically sitting in his lap! It was pretty disgusting, if you ask me."

"Who knew she was such a major flirt?" Kayla asked. "But what I don't get is why she flirted with Jackson, when she's known forever that Lexie likes him. There were a million other guys at the party she could've gone after."

Mr. Whitmore entered the room, and the gossip session was

put on hold. Emma tried to make sense of it. She completely expected Lexie to throw herself at Jackson, especially at a party, but how could Holly go after the one guy Emma liked? She wondered if Shannon and Kayla were telling the truth. Did Ivana put them up to it? She couldn't figure it out.

Out in the hallway after class, Emma overheard two other girls talking about Kayla's party. And Holly throwing herself at Jackson. Then in third-period English class, Sophia Hodges said knowingly to Claire Giberna, "I hear they're a couple now."

"They looked like they'd been a couple forever at the party," Claire said.

Even though the girls didn't say Holly and Jackson's names, Emma knew who they were talking about. The news was clearly all over the school. Was Holly *that* mad at her for not coming to the party that she flirted with Jackson for revenge?

How could she, the one person who knew Emma best, do something so incredibly hurtful in such a public way? Holly had to know it would get back to Emma. Maybe she didn't care. Maybe she'd always had a thing for Jackson but had kept it from Emma. Maybe that's why she wouldn't answer Emma's calls and texts yesterday.

"Where *were* you on Saturday night?" Holly demanded. She was waiting for Emma by their lockers. "I thought you got run over by a hot-dog cart or something."

"That would've been even more convenient than me not showing up, wouldn't it?" Emma met Holly's gaze.

"What are you talking about?" Holly asked, her eyes narrowing.

"How could you not know? The whole school knows you were all over Jackson at Kayla's party."

"Are you kidding me? I wasn't all over Jackson," Holly said.

"That's not the way I heard it. Seems you were in his lap the entire night." Emma could hear her voice growing louder. She and Holly had never fought before, but after everything that had happened over the past couple of months—all the uncomfortable moments and the feeling that they'd never gotten back in their groove after Holly got home from summer vacation—suddenly Emma couldn't stop herself. It was all just spilling out.

"What are you talking about?" Holly demanded. She whipped around and glared at a group of girls in the hall who were not at all subtle about listening in. The girls retreated, giggling and whispering.

"Don't pretend with me. Everyone is talking about how you hooked up with Jackson. Just because I didn't show up—and by the way, I had a very good reason for that—didn't give you the right to do that to me. That's just cruel." Emma took a deep, almost painful, gulp of air. "And I never thought you were cruel."

Holly had a look on her face that Emma had never seen before—a mix of anger, disbelief, and embarrassment maybe—and suddenly Emma worried that they'd just crossed some invisible line. In all their years of friendship, she had never lashed out at Holly like that.

"Wow," Holly finally said. "I can't believe you would accuse me of doing that, especially since I've literally been going out of my way to get you and Jackson together all semester. And you know what else? This was just another time out of maybe like a million that you showed zero effort to be friends with Ivana and the girls—and zero effort to be friends with me. You blew *me* off, Em, so I really don't know who you think *you* are to be mad at *me*."

Emma was stunned. "You are so amazingly selfish!" she cried. She brushed by Holly and practically ran to fourth period.

She didn't stop shaking until the end of seventh period.

By the time the final bell rang, Emma was beyond desperate to escape school and Holly and get to Laceland. She grasped the twenty-dollar bill her mom had slipped her in the hall for a cab. Even her mother knew the importance of an extra fifteen minutes today. Scrambling to shove the right notebooks in her bag at her locker, Emma checked her phone. A text from Paige—no surprise there.

Ms. B: Sending a messenger @ 5pm sharp 2 pick up 3 pieces from ur collection. Model fitting is @ 6. Pls confirm they'll b ready. No margin 4 error. Ciao, PY

"No margin for error," Emma repeated, as she sprinted out the front doors. Wonderful. The last twenty-four hours had been nothing but a study in mess-ups. Her vest was messed up, and now her friendship with Holly was completely messed up. She definitely did not want to add to that growing list.

If the messenger is coming at five o'clock, that only gives me a little more than two hours, she figured. She still needed to check everything—make sure all the loose threads were snipped off and every button was secure—and sew in the Allegra Biscotti labels that she had embroidered with hot-pink thread at home. Plus she had to steam out all of the wrinkles.

She knew she had to get creative and make that corset dress work, because there was no extra time to start over. What she was going to do, she still had no clear idea. Her fingers clenched into fists. This dress could end her dream. She tried to take deep breaths, to push away the suffocating stress so she could create.

Sitting in the backseat of the taxi that blessedly was zipping up Sixth Avenue despite the traffic, Emma psyched herself up. This was the final push. Paint splatters or no paint splatters, she would finish what she started and make it great. Emma typed quickly:

> Ms. Young, Everything will be ready 4 pickup @ 5. Thanks, Allegra Biscotti

"How's it going?" Charlie asked, poking his head into Emma's studio a little while later.

Emma spritzed steam from the handheld steamer near Charlie's face, blasting him with the warm, moist air.

"Not so good, huh?" He blocked his face from another blast of heat.

"Let's be honest here, Charlie. I'm panicking, and I need to focus." Emma turned her attention back to the high, dramatic collar of the dress. Charlie was great but just not now. She had turned Marjorie away earlier, too.

"I'm not even here. Ignore me." He wandered around the room, eyeing each of Emma's finished pieces.

"I will." Emma inspected the zipper running along the back of the dress. She slowly moved it along its tiny tracks, double-checking its grip.

"I heard you and Holls had quite the scene in the hall today—"

"Not now." Emma warned him. What had happened with Holly was too raw, too painful to analyze now. She needed to finish being Allegra first. Then at home quietly, when she was ready, she could figure out what had gone so horribly wrong between her and Holly.

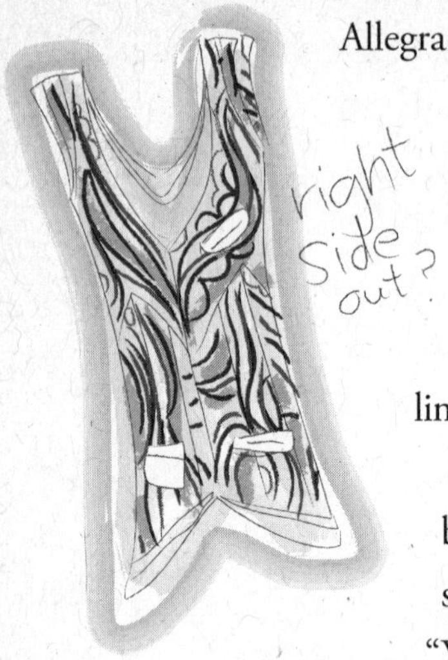

right side out?

After a couple of minutes Charlie said, "Hey, Em, does this lining go all the way around inside?"

She looked up. He was standing by her worktable, the paint-splattered vest in front of him. "Yeah, why?"

"I had an idea. Do you think you could, like, flip it inside out?"

Emma had turned her attention to the dress form now wearing the not-great-enough corset dress. While she still thought of the other dress forms as her "girls," this one seemed more like the hanger-on girl. The girl who worked so hard to fit in with the others, yet everyone else could see that she just didn't have that special something to jell with the group.

"What are you talking about?"

"Well, I mean, the lining is really cool. I actually always liked it better than the outside fabric. So I was thinking: what if you reversed it and made that the outside?"

Dropping the steamer on the table, Emma hurried over to

Charlie's side. She reached for the vest and gently flipped it inside out. She held it away from her body and studied it. It wasn't how she'd originally pictured it at all...but it totally worked.

Now the gorgeous swirly silk lining was on the outside, and the gray silk-jersey fabric peeked out along the edges, as if it had been intended as a border all along. The slit pockets, which she and Marjorie had luckily taken such care to sew, still had their desired effect.

All she had to do was sew the buttons onto the new front, trim the pocket with bits of the gray fabric to counteract the softness of the lining, and add an Allegra Biscotti label to the new inside. No one would ever see the white paint splatters hidden inside.

A huge grin spread from ear to ear as she stripped the never-loved corset dress off the dress form and replaced it with the vest. She stepped back and eyed the three pieces of her original vision together. The printed vest still worked perfectly with the party dress and the structured coat. She raised her arms above her head in triumph.

"Yes! Yes! Charlie! You're a genius!"

For once, Charlie was more modest than usual. "Yes, I am, but you'd probably planned on making it reversible the whole time."

"No, I didn't!" Emma laughed. "I didn't! But who knows... maybe *Allegra* did!"

She eyed the clock. She really had to hurry now to get those buttons on. When she grabbed the tin box off her worktable, she giggled.

"What?" Charlie asked.

Emma held up the box that once had contained biscotti cookies—the very same one that had given Emma the idea for Allegra's last name just three weeks earlier—and shook it. The buttons clanked around inside.

"That has to be a good sign, right?"

"Definitely," Charlie agreed.

allegra B biscotti

He watched as she made the alterations and adjustments to the vest. As she snipped the final threads, he reached behind the filing cabinet and pulled out a large shopping bag. "Here you go."

Inside were three canvas garment bags with the Allegra Biscotti logo that Emma had designed in the upper-left corner of each of them. Emma hugged them to her chest.

"I love them. They're perfect."

"I asked my mom for some of the garment bags she uses to protect her costumes from all those musicals and heat-sealed your logo onto them," Charlie explained. "I thought they'd make everything look more professional and official. Much better than those lame dry-cleaner bags you were going to use."

"Brilliant, as usual." Emma smiled at her friend, and now her partner. "Thank you."

A few minutes later, Marjorie stuck her head into Emma's work space.

"Ready, honey? The messenger from *Madison* is here."

Her dad hurried in, too, not wanting to miss the big moment.

The sensationally cut, sparkly dress with a teasing slit showing a hint of watercolor silk; the fabulously dramatic charcoal jacquard overcoat with its brilliant-striped, pleated lining (and perfect box pleat!); and the dash-of-color vest with gray edges practically danced on their hangers, as if they, too, were eager for their big debut.

Emma zipped up the final bag and turned to Marjorie. "Ready as I'll ever be!"

"I'll take these up front for you, Ms. Biscotti," Marjorie said. She lifted the three garment bags off the garment rack, whisking away Emma's very first collection to face the scrutiny of fashion's top editors.

Emma sunk down onto the stool, her whole body tingling. This was the most exciting, terrifying, satisfying, exhilarating, joyful, and proud moment of her entire life.

This must be what it's like to be a real fashion designer, Emma thought as she followed Charlie and her dad out of her studio and turned off the light: Hurrying and waiting. A million ups and downs. Times when everything was going right and then it...wasn't. Wondering what people would think. Hoping that someone would love what she created as much as she did.

Now there was nothing she could do—no sketching, no sewing, no snipping—but wait.

SURPRISES

Did you hear from her yet?" Charlie asked Emma when he saw her in the hall after sixth period a couple of days later.

"No! No text message or voice mail from Paige. Nothing. The photo shoot supposedly happened yesterday. What do you think that means?" Emma asked. The silence was driving her crazy. Was it good silence, or was it bad silence?

Charlie shrugged. "Who knows?"

Emma sighed. "It's just been such a weird week, you know? I was on this awesome high right after delivering everything to *Madison*. But between not hearing anything from Paige and avoiding Holly, I'm just feeling kind of out of it. Plus, spending every afternoon studying for the Western civ exam is just not as much, I don't know, *fun* as being Allegra."

"I could've told you that, little Miss Split Personality," Charlie said.

"It's just so weird between me and Holly, standing next to each other at our lockers and not talking."

Frustratingly, "Hmm" was all Charlie could muster. For Charlie, Allegra was fascinating and fun. Emma's schoolgirl drama...not so much. She got that she would have to tackle the friendship crisis on her own.

The more she dissected their awful fight, the more she realized that she probably held a lot of the blame. Monday had been a bad and stressful day, and her head had been in Allegra mode, not in Emma mode. Not a choice time to get into it with Holly. Maybe she had overreacted.

What she did know, she decided as another day of mutual silent treatment came to a close, was she wasn't ready to throw away twelve years of the friendship over Ivana or some guy she didn't really know. Some guy who Holly didn't appear to be going out with either, which Emma realized was odd after all of that gossip.

Maybe everybody was wrong, and Holly had been telling the truth. She *knew* Holly. Holly might be a bit caught up in this whole popularity thing, but she most definitely was not a mean, vengeful person.

There must be something I can do to fix this, Emma thought. And soon enough, inspiration struck. She would *stitch* their friendship back together.

The next day, Emma asked Ms. Lyons for a bathroom pass during world history. Rerouting to Holly's locker instead, she spun the combination on Holly's padlock that she had memorized that first day of school—22, the floor that Holly lived on, 18, the floor that Emma lived on, and 37, the reverse of the street Holly lived on.

Emma opened her own locker, pulled out a package wrapped in gold tissue paper and tied with a wine-colored silk cord, and slipped it inside Holly's locker. She had thought about leaving a note but, in the end, decided not to. Holly would either accept the gift as a peace offering, or she wouldn't—but she would definitely know who the package was from and what it meant.

And so Emma spent the rest of the afternoon waiting. Waiting for Paige. Waiting for Holly.

After school, Emma approached her locker as if on tiptoe. Holly was already there, methodically pulling out notebooks and dropping them into her bag. Had their fight been bigger than she thought? Emma wondered.

Holly's body language did not look warm and inviting. Was Holly rejecting her gift—and her friendship? Maybe Emma had gotten so wrapped up with Allegra that she hadn't realized how bad things had truly gotten with Holly.

She twirled her lock, her body feeling as if it was teetering on five-inch spike heels. She couldn't seem to get her balance.

"This is pretty awesome." Holly's voice was low, almost a whisper.

Emma turned slowly. Holly held up the T-shirt Emma had sewn for her the night before. It was a riff on the patchworky-collage design Emma had made out of the vintage music band shirts a few weeks earlier. Emma had sewn a patch out of an old Bazooka gum T-shirt onto a new Swedish cotton long-sleeve crew-neck shirt. And using thick, pink embroidery thread, she had painstakingly embroidered little circles—bubbles—in random spots all over the shirt.

Holly allowed a small smile and then looked down.

Emma shifted awkwardly from foot to foot, not knowing what to do next.

"I'm sorry," she finally said.

"Me, too." Holly smiled widely now.

"You know, Jackson and I aren't a couple," she added. "That was just a nasty rumor."

Emma nodded. "I figured that out. A few days too late..."

"Can I explain what really happened at Kayla's on Saturday night?" Without waiting for answer, Holly continued. "The minute Jackson got there, Lexie started throwing herself at him. It was crazy. So I sort of butted my way in to distract him, so she couldn't completely sink her claws into him. That way you'd be able to talk to him when you got there.

"I knew you didn't really want to come to the party, so I didn't want you to show up and then find Jackson off in a corner with Lexie. But then you never came, so yeah, I guess he and I ended up hanging out most of the night. But it was only so Lexie *wouldn't.* All we did was play Guitar Hero. That's it. Nothing happened between us."

"But what about all the things people were saying?"

"People are idiots," Holly replied. "What's worse is that my friends thought I'd do something like that. Even Ivana and the girls believed what they heard. It didn't matter that they were there and saw for themselves that nothing happened. Em, *nothing* happened. I would *never* do that to you."

"I know that," Emma said quietly. "I really, really do. I'm sorry I didn't give you a chance to explain. And I'm sorry for not coming to the party and for not even letting you know that I wasn't. It was totally rude of me. I wanted to come—I really did—but it turned out to be a crazy weekend. My parents found out that my grades, well, stink, and they grounded me. And you know my mom. She's like the homework police. Going to a party was not happening."

"You were grounded? That's it?" Holly sounded relieved,

almost happy. "Why didn't you just tell me? I thought you didn't come because you didn't like me anymore."

"You made such a big deal about me coming to the party, so it was hard to..." Emma wasn't sure how to finish. She didn't want to upset Holly again.

"I guess I just missed *us*," Holly admitted.

"Me, too," Emma agreed. "Look, I'm sorry about Ivana and the girls getting mad at you, especially because you were looking out for me."

"No, you're not," Holly said with a half smile.

Emma laughed. Holly was right. She wasn't all that sorry about that part.

"But no worries. I spoke to Ivana, and she spoke to Lexie, so we're all cool again," Holly said.

"Oh, um, good," Emma said.

Holly unwrapped a fresh piece of sour green-apple gum and popped it in her mouth. "You know, it used to be so great when it was just you and me. But I really like Ivana and the other girls, too. But I'm not totally clueless, and I know you don't like them."

"Maybe we just have to figure out how to be friends, I don't know, *differently* than we did before," Emma suggested.

Holly nodded. "Definitely, because I really hate the other option, don't you?"

"Totally," Emma agreed. She couldn't imagine her life

without Holly. Holly knew all of Emma's secrets—well, almost all of them.

Emma started to wonder if she should tell Holly about Allegra Biscotti and everything that was happening with *Madison* magazine. Maybe sharing what was really going on for her would help them feel closer again. They had always shared their hopes and dreams.

But something stopped her. Even if I asked Holly not to tell anyone, what would happen if she let something slip to Ivana and the 'Bees, like she did about the sketches of Jackson that day at Bloomingdale's? Did sharing something important and personal with Holly automatically mean that it would get passed along to Ivana? Emma wasn't sure of the answer.

"Whew!" Holly said. "I'm glad that's over. I've had a stomachache the whole week!"

"Me, too!" Emma laughed. Together they examined the bubble gum T-shirt. Emma told Holly all about the cool band tees she'd made, and Holly filled her in on some of the more creative costumes at the party. The halls were almost empty. Emma knew her father would be expecting her at Laceland, but it felt so good to be hanging out with Holly again that she just couldn't leave.

"Hi, Holls. Hi, Emma," cooed a girl's voice.

Emma and Holly lifted their heads to see Lexie walking slowly yet confidently down the hall, hand in hand with Jackson.

"Hey Lex, hey Jackson," Holly said as they passed by.

Emma just gaped. Holly turned toward her. "I'm sorry, Em. I didn't know how to tell you."

"No biggie. He's probably a jerk anyway," Emma said when she found her voice again. But they both knew she still thought Jackson was the furthest thing from a jerk. She couldn't help but be shocked that Jackson went for Lexie. Even though she barely knew him, she had a hard time imagining that Lexie was his type.

Kimono sleeves

textured tights

"Look, I got to go to work. It's part of the grounding deal."

"Okay." Holly looked uncomfortable. "Ivana is supposed to come over later to study. Any chance you want to come, too?"

"Not at all," Emma said with a smile.

"That's what I figured," Holly said, also smiling. "I'll call you tonight."

The girls quickly hugged, then went in their separate directions.

By Friday, Emma still hadn't heard a peep from Paige. Nothing. Silence.

She had spent the week studying and obsessing. She was getting really good at both. She took the Western civilization exam that afternoon. She didn't do perfectly, but she thought she might have done well enough to make it into the class.

She arrived at Laceland a bit later than usual that afternoon. The office was silent.

"Where is everybody?" Emma asked Marjorie as she slid out of her puffy, gold down vest.

Marjorie rolled her lips to evenly distribute the frosted pink lipstick she had just applied and then inspected herself in her hand mirror. "Your dad is at an after-school conference for William, and Isaac's out making deliveries. The phones have been quiet today, too. No important calls, if you know what I mean. How about you?"

Emma frowned. "Nope, not a single one."

"I wouldn't take it to mean anything, honey. People like Paige Young have a limited attention span. They can only focus on the most urgent things in front of them. I'm sure she'll be in touch soon—probably when she needs something." Marjorie stood up to put on her black felt coat. "I'll be back in half an hour."

Emma settled herself in Marjorie's chair. She opened up her bag to see what schoolwork she could get a jump on, so she wouldn't have to spend the entire weekend studying. She and Holly had made plans for Holly to come over and watch a movie on Saturday afternoon—just the two of them—and Emma didn't want there to be any chance that she'd have to cancel. But as she considered her options, she realized that her brain was tired from studying and taking the test. Maybe I'll just color in some of my sketches from this week's rounds of the Game, Emma decided.

She pulled out her sketchbook and then leaned over to dig deeper in her bag to find her pencils, which were all stuck at the bottom. She heard the sound of the front door opening.

Emma lifted her head and almost fell off the chair.

Standing right in front of her, immaculately dressed in a gray wool slim skirt and a deep-purple boat-neck blouse with kimono sleeves, and with her hands on her hips and an unmistakable glare directed at Emma, was Paige Young.

"How was school today, *Allegra?*" Paige asked.

NO LONGER IN THE MARGINS

Emma was too shocked by Paige Young standing in front of her—calling her "Allegra"—to breathe, much less say a single word.

"The look on your face," Paige said coolly, "is pretty much all the proof I need to know that I'm one thousand percent right."

"I…uh…" Emma faltered.

"Wow. *Wow*, I can *not* believe it," Paige said, more to herself than to Emma. "Usually I l-o-v-e being right—it's one of my favorite things—but until a few seconds ago, I was still hoping that perhaps I was wrong about this one. It would've been a whole lot easier if I had been wrong—for the both of us," Paige said, looking right at Emma.

"How did you find out?" Emma asked quietly.

"I hate to tell you, but it wasn't that hard. I had a funny feeling about 'Allegra Biscotti' the whole time, but I kept telling myself that I was just being paranoid since I was going further out on a limb than I'd normally go. Usually I like to—I don't know—*speak* to the designers I'm working with. Call me crazy, but it makes me feel better about them actually existing and all, if you know what I mean.

"Anyway, after I came here looking for Allegra and the receptionist tried to cover up the fact that she had never even heard of Allegra Biscotti, my radar went right up. So I had my assistant call the number you gave me from her cell phone, and you picked up because you didn't recognize the number. I only met you those couple of times, but I did recognize your voice. So voilà—now I'm a fashion detective." Paige laughed ruefully.

"I'm so sorry!" Emma exclaimed, the words now tumbling out. "I didn't mean to trick you. I never in a million years thought it would go this far, but when it did, well, I just couldn't pass up the amazing opportunity you had given me. I wanted to tell you so many times—I really did—but then it felt too late, somehow...but I promise to come clean. I'll tell whoever you want me to tell that it was totally my fault and that you had no idea—"

"Oh, no you won't!" Paige interrupted, bringing her hand down hard on the counter, the back of her huge cushion-cut engagement ring clunking against the Formica surface. "That's *so* not going to happen. You want to know the real reason I didn't pull the plug on this whole thing before? Because all the editors at *Madison*, including yours truly, found

Allegra's—your, whoever's—designs to be fresh and inspired and, well, completely fabulous. Exactly as I anticipated.

"They went absolutely *cray-zee* over your stuff. Would you believe that they actually gave me a hard time about only asking you—Allegra—whomever for three pieces? I had to beat them off with a stick. It was in-SAN-ity."

"Really?" As terrified as Emma was by being confronted by Paige, she couldn't help but be thrilled. The editors of *Madison* magazine loved my designs! Emma thought with delight. They loved them! *Loved* them!

"*Yes, really*. Look, I have too much of my own career as the-editor-who-discovered-this-year's-hottest-new-designer riding on your whole phantom designer house of cards to be ridiculed if people find out Allegra Biscotti is really a—how old are you?"

"Fourteen."

"Is really a fourteen-year-old girl, without a minute of formal training no less! I refuse to become the laughingstock of the fashion industry. I have bigger aspirations than being part of the punch line for a fourteen-year-old's fashion caper. *Much* bigger."

"Oh." Emma looked down at her hands. "I'm sorry. I

really didn't mean to mess up your career or make you look stupid. I would never want that to happen. Allegra can just disappear. Maybe someday we can—"

Paige rapped on the counter with her knuckles to make Emma stop blabbering and look up. "Um, hello? I don't think you're quite picking up what I'm laying down here. Allegra is not going *anywhere*—especially not disappearing without a trace. Allegra is only just beginning.

"Here's the deal: I'm planning to keep the secret until they pry it out of my cold, dead hands and you—and whoever else knows—must swear-swear-swear to keep it as well. And because you have a bonkers amount of talent—and because I happen to be a very nice person—I'll help Allegra Biscotti as a sort of mentor.

"I'll give you my advice and share my professional insight, as long as you don't blow our cover. And, of course, I'll expect you to give me and *Madison* exclusive coverage. Do we have a deal or what?" Paige reached her hand across the counter.

Emma grabbed her hand and shook it vigorously. "Are you kidding? Definitely! You can count on me. I'm pretty good at keeping secrets. Not too many people know about Allegra. My best friend doesn't even know!" Emma rambled on with relief, "Wow. I can't believe you're going to help me! That's so amazing. You have the best taste in the world and must know everyone in the business!"

Paige allowed a proud smile. "True and true. But I mean it," she said, wagging her index finger at Emma, "this one goes in the vault. Got it?"

"Totally," Emma said, a grin spreading from ear to ear. "Thank you, thank you, thank you!"

"Good. Now, as your official mentor, here's my first piece of advice: for the love of Gucci, buy a new cell phone for Allegra Biscotti with a different phone number. My second piece of advice is to set up an Allegra Biscotti Web page with an email address. We're about to enter the big leagues here. No more kiddie texting stuff, got it? I'm not about to stick my neck out when there's the risk of you picking up your cell phone as you and not Allegra and blowing it with one slip of the fabric shears."

"Gotcha," Emma agreed.

"Once those things are done, I'll give out Allegra's number and email address to some select people in New York, who could help get Allegra's designs seen and worn by the right people. And then, watch out! I predict that this thing is going to explode, like huge. So get ready."

"I'm ready," Emma said. "I've been getting ready for this moment my whole life. It just came a lot sooner than I thought it would."

"I'll be in touch," Paige said, spinning on her heel to

leave. Suddenly, she turned back toward Emma. "You did an amazing job, by the way. I have to admit I'm even more impressed with the work now that I know the truth. I brought Polaroids from the shoot to show you."

She unsnapped a cocoa leather clutch that looked so buttery soft Emma wanted to stroke it, and she pulled out a stack of photos.

"We love, love, loved that everything was reversible. Genius. Twice the bang for the buck! We shot each piece both ways, and the model was raving about how comfortable everything was, which never happens. Models don't rave."

Looking at snapshots of a lanky, gorgeous model in her designs sent Emma reeling from her body. She hovered, peering over Paige's perfectly casual bun at her designs. Which looked...fabulous!

"The vest had a tiny spot or two on the inside. We don't know how it happened, and we'll pay to have it cleaned. We have the *best* cleaner...there's not a spot on earth that Felix can't get out. For the shoot, we just styled it with this over-the-top chunky turquoise deco pin. To die for, isn't it?" she asked, holding out the photo for Emma to see. And yes, thought Emma, it was to die for.

"Gotta run," Paige said, as she shuffled the photos together, deposited them into her clutch, and snapped it shut in one swift motion. "*Ciao* for now."

Emma just stood there, smiling. And the smile was still on her face when she fell into bed exhausted, relieved, and oh, so happy that night.

By the next week, Emma felt like her life had pretty much returned to normal, at least on the outside. It was almost as if she had dreamed the whole thing—but inside, she felt completely different. Like a fairy godmother had waved a magic wand and changed her life—forever.

But life at Downtown Day hadn't changed.

Emma caught herself still sneaking a peek at Jackson every few minutes during world history. He looked great today, as usual. The royal blue in his flannel plaid shirt made his eyes stand out even more than usual. How was she supposed to just shut off her feelings for him now that he was officially going out with Lexie Blackburn?

I have to, she told herself, because by the looks of all the hand-holding going on lately, he's clearly interested in Lexie and not me.

But a few minutes later, Emma's mind wandered away from what Ms. Lyons was saying once again. She noticed that Jackson was drawing furiously in his notebook. For the billionth time, Emma wished she could see what he was doing. Oh well, she told herself, now that he's with Lexie, that's never going to happen. She forced herself to return her attention to the lesson. There was a test at the end of the week.

The bell finally rang. Emma stood and then looked down to shove her textbook back in her bag. She swung around to leave and then—crash! She and Jackson smashed right into each other. Emma fell sideways, grabbing the desk for support. Jackson lost his balance and landed right back in his chair, dropping his notebook as he went down.

Emma scrambled to stand. "I'm so sorry! That was totally my fault. I wasn't looking."

Jackson seemed stunned for a second. Then he shook it off. "You okay?"

"Yeah, I'm fine." She leaned down, picked up his notebook, and as she handed it back to him, she felt the same jolt of excitement she had experienced at the school assembly—something electric. And unless Emma was imagining it, the half-smile on Jackson's face made Emma think that he had felt it, too.

"Thanks," he said, taking the notebook back with one hand as he reached up to push his hair away from his forehead with his other.

Suddenly feeling bold, Emma asked, "Can I see what you've been drawing? I mean, I just happened to notice that you spent most of class drawing something, and I was just...curious."

Jackson looked surprised but not angry or insulted. He scanned the classroom. Most everyone had already left, leaving the room empty except for the two of them and a couple of kids talking with Ms. Lyons up at her desk. He opened his notebook and leaned toward Emma so only she could see. Their shoulders were almost touching.

The margins of the pages were filled with the most amazing comic-book art. "Wow. So cool."

"You draw and stuff, right?" Jackson asked.

"Yeah." Now it was Emma's turn to be surprised. She instinctively patted the sketch pad tucked away in her bag. She had no idea that Jackson had noticed that she drew. All this time she'd thought she was the one staring at him.

"And you really think this is good?" he asked, his face open and vulnerable.

Emma couldn't believe he was asking for *her* opinion. "Totally. I really like what you've done with the style. It's bold and simple—in a good way, I think, because it's not too detailed or busy. I also like the way the characters seem to jump off the pages, like they're three-dimensional. See, here?" She pointed to figure of a guy holding a book in one hand and a sword in the other. "He's totally great. He looks like someone we'd know but also a hero at the same time."

"Exactly!" Jackson said enthusiastically. "That's what I was going for!"

At that moment, Lexie appeared in the doorway to the classroom.

"Hey, Jackson! I've been waiting for you at your locker." Lexie was wearing a dress so short that Emma was positive it was meant to be a shirt. Even so, she looked beyond amazing in it. "Come on!"

Jackson closed his notebook and gathered the rest of his stuff. Emma put her bag down on the desk and pretended to reorganize her things. He started to make his way over to meet Lexie, waiting impatiently at the door. Then he stopped and ripped a page from his notebook. He handed it to Emma without a word. In a few long strides, he was out the door with Lexie. Emma could hear her giggles echoing down the hall, the sound slowly fading into general hallway chatter.

Emma closed her eyes to let the Jackson "moment" sink in. When she opened them again, she looked down at the page he had given her. It was the drawing of the hero that she especially liked. Emma tucked it into her own sketchbook for safekeeping—right between her own sketches of Allegra Biscotti's next collection.

Here's a sneak peek at

The Allegra Biscotti Collection #2: Who, What, Wear

Emma grabbed the pink smocked child's dress. "Think your mom would mind if I took this?"

"Are you kidding? She won't even notice. Take it." Holly smiled. "I'll text you later."

Moments later, as Emma walked down the hushed, carpeted hallway of Holly's apartment building, she replayed what had just happened. Holly had seemed sincerely willing to turn down Ivana's invitation if Emma wanted. But she hadn't exactly tried to change her mind when she'd offered to leave either. So was this how it was going to be between them?

Once inside the elevator, Emma tucked the child's dress into her black canvas messenger bag, which she had decorated with Klimt-like designs, and pulled out her sketchbook. By the time the doors slid open in the lobby, she had the sweet dress halfway redesigned into a chic modern mini. Her feet automatically carried her down the sidewalk of Holly's tree-lined Upper Eastside street toward the nearest subway station. She slid out her cell phone and dialed.

"Yo," Charlie Calhoun's familiar voice answered on the second ring.

"Hi," Emma said. "What's up? Are you working on the site?"

"I've been slaving away all day. The people at Tome probably think I've moved in permanently."

Emma smiled, picturing him sitting at one of the rickety, mismatched tables in their favorite funky little hole-in-the-wall independent bookstore, creating a website for Allegra Biscotti. "Thanks for doing this. You know computer stuff puts me to sleep even faster than math class."

"You stick to the fashion, I'll take care of the tech."

"Sounds like a plan. I—" Emma stopped short as she heard a buzzing from inside her bag. What was that? The buzz sounded again, and suddenly the answer hit her. "Oops, hold on a sec," she told Charlie, jamming her cell between her cheek and her shoulder, as she reached into her bag. "The Allegra phone's ringing."

Along with the new website, Paige had ordered Emma to get a separate phone. It was important to keep her Emma-life separate from her new Allegra-life. Yesterday after school Emma and Charlie had picked out a sleek cherry-colored flip phone that seemed perfect for Allegra. This was the first time it had rung. She would definitely have to find a new ringtone!

"Hold on, hold on," she muttered as she dug deeper into her bag, searching for the phone as it buzzed again. "Where are you?"

"What?" Charlie's voice drifted into her ear.

"Not talking to you." Emma twisted her head around, trying not to drop her own phone as she kept groping for the other. Why hadn't she put Allegra's phone in the little pouch where she kept hers?

No, forget that. She knew the answer. Allegra was a secret. How was she supposed to explain having two cell phones if someone like Holly noticed?

"Hey! Watch it!"

Emma glanced up just in time to avoid running into a pair of nannies pushing matching double-baby strollers. "Um, sorry," she mumbled, darting around the strollers while four sets of wide baby eyes stared at her with fascination.

The Allegra phone was still buzzing insistently, again and again, sounding slightly muffled. Who was on the phone? Could she be missing the biggest fashion opportunity of her career?

Emma frantically yanked her world history textbook out of the bag, dropping it to the sidewalk at her feet. It crashed against the concrete, sounding like a gunshot, causing at least two of the babies that had just passed to wail. The nannies sent Emma a dirty look as they pushed the strollers away faster.

"I just remembered," Charlie shouted through the phone she still held awkwardly to her ear by her shoulder, "I never set the Allegra phone to voice mail."

"Yeah, I kind of figured that out after the eleventh ring!" Emma said. "I'm calling you back." She shoved her phone into her vintage paisley-print coat pocket.

She pulled more stuff out of her bag. The pink smocked dress. Her sketchbook. Some jewel-toned fabric scraps she'd rescued from the trash at Allure. The cool graphic wrapper from a European candy bar. A half-finished set of math problems. An interesting brocade fan she'd picked up in Chinatown. More fabric—this time a sample of a funky new geometric-print twill she wanted to find a way to use. Was this a messenger bag or a clown car? Suddenly all Holly's teasing about her keeping her whole life in the messenger bag didn't seem so funny—or so professional.

Finally her hand closed on the cool metal of Allegra's phone. She snatched it from the bottom of the bag. "Hello?" she said breathlessly, as a young boy glided by on a skateboard, staring curiously at the pile of random stuff at her feet. "Uh, Allegra Biscotti's office?"

"Emma?" a voice barked out. "That you?"

Emma gulped, feeling a familiar rush of nerves. "Hi, Paige. Yes, it's me. So you got the new phone number I emailed you, huh? That's good, I—"

"Listen, I don't have much time—I'm already five minutes late for a production meeting," Paige interrupted, talking at warp speed. "But I wanted to touch base with you before I go in. You probably already heard that *Madison* is going to be sponsoring a super-amazing pop-up shop here in the city next month, right?"

"Um, no?" Emma felt slightly stupid. Sometimes she suspected that Paige forgot she was only fourteen and still pretty new to the big-time fashion world.

"It's going to be huge, huge, huge," Paige said. "It'll only be open for one weekend—like the flash mob of pop-ups." She barked out a laugh. "The press is already eating it up."

"Sounds cool." Emma wasn't sure why Paige was in a rush to tell her all this if she was running so late. She could hear the echo of Paige's stilettos click-clacking double-time down a hallway.

Her bag suddenly slipped off her shoulder, and Emma automatically grabbed at it, almost dropping her phone. Catching the phone just in time, she shifted it to her other ear and missed part of whatever Paige said next.

"...schedule is tight, and there isn't a minute to lose, but it'll all be worth it," Paige was saying. "This is going to be huge for Allegra! As in, gigantic! No, bigger than that!"

Emma stared blindly out at the traffic passing on Lexington Avenue as she tried to follow what Paige was saying. "Um, what is?" she asked tentatively.

"Are you deaf?" Paige sounded impatient. "My boss just agreed that Allegra Biscotti's holiday line is going to be featured in our Choice New Designers pop-up shop! You're going to be a star! This is it, Emma. Make-it or break it time for Allegra Biscotti."